The Neighbors

A Christian Christmas Romance

By

Karen Cogan

SIGN UP FOR MY NEWSLETTER for news, freebies ands fun and
get a free download of my sweet contemporary romance MADE FOR
EACH OTHER

SCAN HERE

CHAPTER ONE

Abby parted the brocade curtains at the living room widow and peered out. Grimacing, she said, "I knew I heard something. That boy is at it again. He's shrieking and bouncing his ball against the side of his house. I don't know how the next-door neighbor stands it. She ought to call the police and have them talk to his mother."

Vic shifted in the overstuffed armchair and lowered the newspaper. "I don't hear anything. So, maybe it doesn't bother the neighbor. If it bothers you, report it as a public nuisance."

She shook her head at the man who'd been her husband for almost fifty years. "I don't want someone that inconsiderate to know I called the police. The noise doesn't bother you because you don't hear much of anything even with your hearing aids."

"What haven't I paid?"

She replied, "I said hearing aids, not paid."

Then she noticed his grin. "Very funny. How about we have lunch? I have leftover egg salad if you want some."

Vic cocked his head, "Did you say lonesome? There's a little room in the chair if you don't mind squeezing in."

Abby chuckled as she studied him. "Stop it, you old goose. You know what I said."

"Yep. The egg salad sounds good, but so does a cuddle. Come on over here sit still a minute. You flit around so much you make me tired."

Abby slid onto his lap. "Let me know if I hurt you."

Vic put his arm around her waist. "You don't weigh more than a thistle. I think my old legs can take it."

Abby sighed. Sitting like this reminded her of their courtship and early marriage when they cuddled for hours on the sofa. Where had all that time gone and how did they get so old? They had changed so much over the years that she would hardly recognize them from their wedding pictures. Of course, it happened to everyone, she simply didn't think it would happen so fast.

She sat with Vic for a few minutes before using the armrests to shove herself to her feet. "Okay. Up, now. You need to eat so I can get your noon meds into you."

"Lunch. Then a nap," Vic said.

"You sleep so much you remind me of a hibernating bear."

"Like I said, you should slow down. You work too hard. There's not a spot of dust anywhere in this place. You could rest with me today."

"I'll join you after a bit. There's some baking I want to do first. I want to get the cookies shipped before the grandkids start their finals. Nibbling on them helps them concentrate. "

Vic patted his amble waist. "They help me put on weight."

"I'll have them boxed before you wake up."

"If you left out two or three, I shouldn't think that would hurt me," Vic said.

"You'll have to eat them after supper, so you don't raise your blood sugar too fast," Abby said.

They ate lunch in the same leisurely manner that defined their activities these days. Abby spooned egg salad from the refrigerator over the toasted bread. She gave them each a cup of applesauce and glasses of cold iced tea and they sat at the round dinette table to eat.

Abby had not pushed aside the curtains on the window near the table. The view of the ornamental plum tree with pretty foliage in spring; summer, and fall, was barren and brown in winter. It depressed her.

She sighed. Her optimism failed her this winter. Vic was too sedentary and tired to want to go out and trips to the grocery store were her main social outlet unless one of their daughters called for a chat.

She longed for the days when she'd baked Christmas cookies for her girls to take to their teachers and neighborhood friends. Downsizing to a smaller house had been a must and the cul-de-sac was quiet except for the boy who bounced his tennis ball against the wall or came out to shout when he was angry.

She shook her head. She would never have tolerated such a child.

God had blessed her with two daughters. They were good students and hardly ever a worry with them. She regretted they lived on opposite sides of the country. Linda had settled on the west coast and Julie taught in a university in Connecticut. Abby and Vic rarely saw Julie's two girls who were nearing their teenage years and Linda had no kids. For a while, Vic and Abby had considered moving to Connecticut but decided to stay in their hometown where they had friends and doctors they liked.

Vic broke into her thoughts.

"After my nap, I thought we might give the girls a call. We can see what they're doing for Christmas."

Abby sighed. "I'd love to talk to them, but you'll try to talk them into coming for the holidays and they've already said they can't. It makes them feel guilty."

Vic held up two fingers. "I won't say a word. I promise."

Abby doubted he'd keep his promise. Yet she did want to talk to the girls.

"All right. We'll see if we can get them."

Vic dished out a little more egg salad and chewed the bites slowly before he finally licked the spoon. Abby wished he'd hurry so she could get to the store and finish before the afternoon rush when moms stopped off after school with their kids.

When Vic trudged off for his nap, Abby washed the dishes before she grabbed her list and purse and headed for the store. As she pulled from the driveway, she glanced behind her to see the irritating boy's mom slam her car door and roar from the driveway nearly clipping Abby's rear fender.

Abby braked hard and did a quick intake of breath. She stared at the car as it disappeared onto the next street. What was wrong with the woman? She was as thoughtless as her son.

Abby had nearly forgotten the incident when she got to the store. Fortunately, it wasn't crowded. As she made her way from the vegetable aisle to the meats, she realized smells were beginning to bother her. By the time she got the deli meat, her stomach was rolling. The sweet scents from the bakery mingled with the pungent aroma of salami and cheese.

She hurried to check out and exited the store. Waves of nausea accompanied her drive home. The road rose and roiled in front of her in time with her stomach.

"Merry Christmas," she whispered.

Her plans to bake Christmas cookies today and ship them tomorrow for the grandkids were ruined. She swallowed over a lump in her throat.

The holidays didn't look promising. She wasn't going to see the kids. Vic never wanted to go out anymore and she felt crummy. It wasn't a good start to the holidays.

She opened the trunk to take in the groceries and realized she didn't have the strength.

Vic glanced up from the couch as she staggered into the house. One look at her face must have told all. He shoved himself up and took her arm. "What's wrong, honey?"

"It's my stomach. It feels terrible."

"Let's get you to bed. I hope you don't have the flu. I heard it's going around."

Nausea clawed at her throat and she leaned on Vic as they headed to the bedroom. He propped up her pillow and sat her onto the bed to remove her shoes. She sank against the pillow as he lifted her legs onto the bed.

"Would you like a soda?" Vic asked.

Abby shook her head. "No. My stomach is too upset. I just want to close my eyes."

"You do that, honey. I'll sit in the chair and read. You tell me if you need anything."

Abby nodded. The ache in her bones caused her to long for pain relief, yet she didn't think she could keep down any medicine. She drifted to sleep and awoke a while later to find that Vic wasn't in the room. She shivered and drew the cover tighter around her. Her mouth was too dry to swallow so she called out to Vic to bring her some water.

He appeared a moment later. "You're awake. I was just coming back to check on you."

"Would you bring me a glass of water?" Abby asked.

"Of course. Do you want ice in it?"

Abby shook her head." I'm too cold."

Vic disappeared and returned with a glass of tepid water. Abby sipped it slowly, so she didn't upset her stomach. After a few swallows, she handed it to Vic to set on the nightstand.

"I was putting away our groceries," Vic said. "I didn't think about you having them in the trunk until a neighbor stopped by and told me she saw them. The nice young lady insisted on helping me carry them inside."

Abby winced. "I was so miserable I forgot about them. Did anything melt?"

Vic shook his head. "We got to them in time."

"Who was it that helped you?"

"I forget her name. She lives next door to the boy that makes you so mad."

"I told you she must be a saint," Abby mumbled before she fell back asleep.

CHAPTER TWO

Krista had waved to the old man as he shut the door. Should he and his wife be living alone? He'd said his wife felt sick when she got home from the store and that was why she forgot about the groceries. Krista hoped he could take care of her. She'd given him her phone number in case they needed a meal. Hopefully, they would call and not be as independent as her grandparents had been. They were married fifty-two years before Grandpa died two years ago. They should have been in assisted living yet refused to go. Grandma had finally made that move a year ago. She had made new friends and she spoke with Mom every day to reminisce.

Krista blinked back tears. There was a history of long marriages in her family. Mom and Dad celebrated twenty-five years recently. Six months ago, Krista thought she'd found the right someone and that she would have a long and happy marriage. She'd been wrong She shook the thought away as she continued home.

Dusk fell early this time of year, especially on a cloudy evening. A few flakes of snow fell on the way to her house. When she got inside the one-story bungalow, she brewed a cup of hot tea and thought back over her day. Surgical assistance had taken up most of her time. Then, she'd filled out paperwork until time to go home. Now she had an evening to fill.

She decided to get out the Christmas decorations. Though she didn't have many, she cherished the few she'd kept from childhood. The foot-high ceramic tree would light her coffee table and the stuffed puppy with a Santa hat would play Jingle Bells. She would place the wreath with a red velvet bow and tiny presents wrapped in shiny foil on the outside of the front door. Most precious of all was the glass snow globe that dropped snow on the little house with a tinseled Christmas tree in the front yard. The base of the globe showed the inside of the house with children sleeping in the bedrooms and Santa coming down the living room chimney.

Krista loved Christmas with all her heart. She hoped one day she would have children to share the faith and traditions she cherished. Whether this would happen seemed uncertain and this year she would spend Christmas with her parents and her grandmother.

Her cell buzzed. It was Becky from work. She sounded breathless." Have you heard?"

"Heard what?"

"Some nut shot the security guard at the information desk today. Fortunately, it was a shoulder wound and not fatal."

Krista nearly dropped the phone. "Why in the world...?"

"I heard the husband was mad that his wife's ex made it into her hospital room after he left. Did you happen to see the husband after his wife's surgery today?"

Krista thought over her day. "No, I don't think I did."

"With violence like that, I don't feel safe anymore."

"People can be kinda crazy when they get mad," Krista said.

"I guess they have to have someone to blame," Becky said.

"At least we didn't have to deal with him. I'm glad of that."

When they hung up, Krista sat on the sofa. She'd planned on having dinner and then putting out the decorations. Now, a portion of her Christmas cheer evaporated as she wondered if any job was safe anymore. She stroked the stuffed puppy with the Santa hat and longed for the innocence of childhood when she'd felt safe and protected and didn't know about evil or danger.

After a while, she got off the sofa. She was drawn to the aroma coming from the kitchen. Since Krista rarely used the stove or oven, the green, paisley, crock-pot was her best friend. Tonight, it held ribs she'd smothered with barbecue sauce in the morning. Salad and French bread would complete the meal.

She lifted the lid and inspected the dark meat swimming in a red, spicy, sauce. She sliced the bread and pulled leaves off lettuce before adding chopped carrots and celery.

With her plate fully loaded, she settled on the sofa and flipped through channels looking for a Christmas movie. She smiled when she stumbled upon Miracle on 34th Street. The faith of the little girl always inspired her. Perhaps a miracle romance would be possible for Krista.

The movie was still playing when she finished eating. She put her dishes in the sink and began to decorate while listening to the background sound of the movie. She plugged in the ceramic tree and placed it and the snow globe on the coffee table. The stuffed Santa puppy grinned from his seat atop the end table beside the couch. All that was left was placing the wreath outside the door.

Krista grimaced at the icy wind that rushed in when she hung the wreath on the hook that had waited an entire year for the return of the ornament. Though the decorating of this house was complete, Krista was not finished with her holiday bedecking. Tomorrow evening, she would help her mom and dad pick a tree that would drip with colored balls, homemade ornaments, and tinsel. The finished product would not look like the carefully crafted trees in movies or in magazines. Yet, Krista cherished the evidence of their history as a family. Each of Krista's elementary school ornaments, as well as the many others her mother had received from students, held precious memories. Was it possible these memories might displace the ache in her heart? Time would tell. Yet time seemed to have crawled to a halt.

The next morning Krista raised the kitchen blinds and saw a dusting of snow covering the backyard. Sunlight gave it the sparkle of thousands of diamonds. Though she'd never liked to drive on it, she admired the pristine beauty of a fresh downfall.

She carried her cup of coffee to the bedroom to sip while she dressed in slacks and a crisp white blouse. Calf-length leather boots would keep her feet dry on the trek from the parking lot into the hospital.

Her thoughts flashed to the conversation with Becky last night. The assault on the security guard seemed incongruous with the Christmas season. At this time of peace and good cheer, it was a reminder that the world was not always a safe or kind place. As she locked the front door, a shiver from inner disquiet rather than frigid air shook her.

The boy next door was out, scooping up handfuls of snow and throwing it into the air. Bald patches of withered grass now disrupted the beauty of the scene. She wasn't surprised by his spoiling of the beauty. Now that he was off for Christmas break, she dreaded the extra noise and commotion. Last year, he broke two of her windows. She didn't want to imagine what mischief he would get into now that he was a year older.

She drove slowly down the frosty street until she reached the hospital. She parked in a reserved spot and slid from the car while pulling her coat more tightly around her as she scurried to the entrance. The two women who worked the information desk greeted her as usual. The hallway looked as peaceful as it did every morning. She could hardly believe the drama that had occurred the previous evening. She would never feel completely safe inside the hospital again.

After an uneventful day of work, when Krista arrived home, a little dog ran across the street and followed her up to her house. She looked down at the dog. "You can't come in with me."

The creature looked at her with soft brown eyes. Its silky ears were soft, velvet, ovals that lay along its golden wavy fur. Though Krista had not been raised with dogs, this one's endearing expression might have convinced her to pet it if she'd been sure it wouldn't bite.

"You need to go home."

The dog ignored her firm tone and continued to stare up at her as though waiting for her to open the door for them.

"You can't come in," Krista repeated.

The dog hopped up the step and whined.

Krista sighed. The man who owned this dog lived in the gray brick house. He wasn't at the front door and the garage remained closed. Krista shivered in the cold as she stared at the house in hopes the man might and come out to seek his pet.

Five minutes later, the frigid air had seeped into her bones and she longed to go into her warm house. "We have to do something," she muttered. "We can't stand here all night. Let's see if you'll follow me across the street."

Krista walked backwards toward the street. "Come on. This way"

The dog followed her. Its bobbed tail wagged back and forth as it headed home.

What am I going got do if he's not here? Krista wondered. She couldn't leave the creature out in the cold to wander and get lost. Oh please, be home.

She rang the bell and waited. When the porch light flicked on and bathed them in its glow, she breathed a sigh of relief. The man opened the door and his curious expression changed to surprise. He stared at his dog. "Angel, what are you doing out here, girl?"

"She followed me to my front door," Krista said.

He stood aside and Krista caught a whiff of a meaty Mexican supper."

The man stuck out his hand. "I'm Trent. Thanks for bringing her home. Would you like to come in and warm up? I've got supper on the stove. You're welcome to stay."

Krista panicked This was more interaction than she'd planned. "I can't tonight but thanks for asking. I'm glad you were home. I wasn't sure what to do with Angel."

He grinned at her and a dimple appeared. His dark eyes lit with amusement. "It appears she would have come into your house, plopped down, and waited for her supper."

"I don't have any dog food."

He chuckled. "Whatever you were eating would have been fine with her. She's a beggar."

"I'm glad I could bring her home, but I better go," she said.

His charm unsettled her. She hadn't expected to have this dark-haired, attractive man open the door. She'd only seen him from a distance. Up close, he was muscular and handsome.

"I'll try to keep her home," he said.

"No problem."

She turned and chugged through the frosty night toward home. The twinkling of a thousand stars beamed down at her in amusement at her emotions. She would rather have been cloaked in darkness. No matter, she could not hide from the emotions churning inside her. His lanky ease when he'd spoken and the light in his eyes stuck in her memory.

Forget it. He doesn't even know my name. I won't see him for months. Then, it will only be when he comes out to mow his grass. Was she disappointed? No. It was ridiculous.

She barely tasted the soup she heated. However, by the time she turned on the Christmas music and settled with her novel, she'd almost forgotten Trent.

Saturday morning was so chilly Krista was in no hurry to get out of bed. She finally wrapped herself in her fuzzy chenille bathrobe and headed to the kitchen for a mug of hot coffee. As she sat at her tiny table, she pondered her day. Maybe she should check on the elderly couple down the block. Maybe they needed something from the store. Krista planned to make a trip, anyway.

She took another hour to dress in jeans and a warm green sweatshirt adorned with silver jingle bells and to make two scrambled eggs. She ate them while she sat at the table and penned a grocery list.

The doorbell rang. She hopped up wondering who could be at her door at eleven o'clock on a Saturday morning. She looked out the peep hole to see Trent and her heart froze. She hadn't brushed her hair yet or put on any make-up.

He rang again. She moved away from the peep hole though he couldn't possibly see her. Her heat raced while she stood frozen to the floor. There was no way was she answering the door when she looked such a frump.

A few moments later, she peered out to see that he had gone away. A wave of disappointment broke her anxiety. He'd been charming last night. He had a friendly easiness that she admired. Still, she had not been ready for him this morning. Maybe, she'd have a chance to wave at him if they were out at the same time.

She straightened the house and ate a light lunch before she headed out the door to go to the store. She stopped in front of the house next door to check on how the older woman was feeling. It took some time before her husband opened the door. His heavy breathing made her wonder if he'd been doing chores.

"I hope I'm not interrupting. I came by to see if you need anything at the store," Krista said.

"I'll ask my wife. She's feeling better today."

"I'm so glad. Don't let her overdo it. She seemed pretty sick."

"I'm keeping a good eye on her. She does the same thing for me."

"It's good you have each other."

"Yes. It is. I couldn't manage without her."

He motioned to Krista. "Come inside while I ask if we need anything."

Krista stepped into the foyer and closed the door. The house had a homey feel. The sitting room to the left held a piano and cozy floral settee. She wondered which of them played the piano. Krista loved music and she loved playing the piano.

Ahead of her, the foyer opened into a living room. She couldn't see the entire room. A mounted television on the wall and a coffee table that she supposed sat in front of a couch was all she could see.

When the man returned, he said, "We're all good for the store. She bought enough before she got sick to last us for this week. Thanks for checking, though."

"It's my pleasure. Be sure and let me know if anything comes up and you need help."

He nodded. "Will do. She's going to miss not having our of kids around for Christmas but there's not much we can do about that."

"I suppose not," Krista agreed. "My parents always assume I'll be there."

"They're fortunate you live in the same town."

"So am I. I'd miss them if I didn't."

The man smiled. "It's good to have family nearby. You have a good day and don't worry about us."

"Okay. I'll see you soon."

She drove to the store. The car warmed to a comfortable cocoon by the time she arrived. The store was crowded with Christmas shoppers stocking up for holiday baking. A wave of nostalgia swept over Krista. She remembered making dozens of cookies with Mom every Christmas. The smell of gingerbread and sweet icing filled the house. Maybe she'd surprise Mom with a pan of gingerbread tonight. Krista mentally added molasses to her list. When she found everything she needed, she joined the line of holiday shoppers at the checkout. She hoped she hadn't forgotten anything because returning and waiting in line again would take a large chunk of time.

After she got home, she put away the groceries and started on the gingerbread. She'd just gotten it in the oven when the doorbell rang. She looked out to see Trent standing on the porch. Though a surge of adrenalin surged through her veins again, she felt more presentable than she had in the morning.

She opened the door and greeted him.

He grinned in return. "I'm sorry for coming by unannounced. I don't have your number."

"That's okay. Won't you come in?"

He stepped into the foyer and held out a small Christmas gift bag with pictures of angels on the outside. She looked from the gift to his face. "Oh my. What is this for?"

He smiled at her. "It's for bringing my Angel back last night. "

She stammered. "It's something any neighbor would have done. You didn't need to bring me a gift."

"I know. I wanted to."

She dug inside and brought out a beautiful Christmas angel made of glass. The angel held a harp and had a cord for hanging on a tree. Krista gasped at the breathtaking treasure.

"She's beautiful. Thank you."

"I'm glad you like it. It will make you remember me and Angel when you see it."

"Yes. It will. I have gingerbread baking in the oven. It will be done in fifteen minutes. Would you like me to bring some over?"

"I'd love that. If you have time, I could stay and chat until it's baked, but I don't want to take time if you don't have it. By the way, what's your name? I figured since we're neighbors, it's okay to ask."

"It's Krista."

"That's pretty."

"Thank you." Her stomach tightened with nervous anticipation. Yet, she did want him to stay.

She asked, "Would you like some coffee? We can sit in the living room while we wait for the gingerbread."

He grinned. "I'd like that."

She started the coffee and joined him on the floral sofa that was a hand me down from her parents. It had no holes, and the springs were good. It was hardly even faded. Being an only child had its advantages sometimes. She had been able to move her bedroom furniture and piano into the house also. The only thing she'd had to buy was the television and a tiny dining table."

Trent glanced around the room. "I like your art. Did you take the photos?"

"No. My dad did. He's an amateur photographer. When I was a kid, we visited all the major national parks and when I got this apartment, he framed photos of them for me."

"I'm impressed. What do you do for a living?"

She shrugged. "Nothing glamorous. I'm a surgical nurse."

"That sounds impressive to me. I was never good with blood or needles. I'm the owner of a construction company."

A giggle escaped from her. "I thought I should take a woodworking class in middle school. I made a "C" because the teacher took pity on me. I made "A"s" in my other subjects."

He grinned at her. "You can't be good at everything."

She parried back. "How were your grades?"

He groaned. "Don't ask."

Rising, she said, "I'm going to get the coffee and we'll talk about things other than our failures."

"Good idea. I bet I can guess what sort of movies you enjoy."

She laughed. "Bet you're wrong."

She returned with steaming coffee in colorful reindeer mugs. He accepted his and thanked her. She settled on the sofa and was less nervous now that they'd broken the ice,

"Now about movies," he said. "I think you like a heartfelt drama where someone gets their heart broken, but there is a happy ending at the end. Am I right?"

"Not even close. Give me an action movie with danger and daring escapes. There's enough drama in life without watching it in movies."

"Seriously? I like those, too. A good suspense movie or spy thriller is the best."

"I think so, too.

They chatted for a bit before she excused herself to get the gingerbread out of the oven. She returned with two steaming servings. He took the plate with an appreciative smile. "I love the smell and taste of gingerbread. I think most of us associate it with Christmas."

Krista settled with her slice. "I know I do. This recipe came from my grandmother. I remember walking into her house the week before Christmas and eating it with hot cocoa."

He took a sip of coffee before answering. "It seems we have similar tastes. There's an action movie that just came out that I've wanted to see. Would you consider going with me?"

Her pulse quickened. This handsome man was asking for a date. "That would be fun. When were you thinking of going?"

"Are you free tonight?"

I'm afraid not. I promised my parents I'd help them pick out and decorate a tree."

What about next week? I'm free most nights."

"Tuesday?" She asked.

He sat his empty mug on a coaster. "That's perfect. I think the movie is still showing at seven o'clock next week. Does that work?"

She fell into the depths of his blue eyes and mentally rearranged her Christmas shopping plans. "It works fine."

"Should I come over at six-forty to get you? It's not far to the show."

"I can be home and ready by then."

His grin showed his dimple. "Good. I should let you get back to your day since I interrupted you unexpectedly."

"I enjoyed the interruption. Straightening the house was next on my to-do list. You gave me an excuse to put it off."

"Let me help you straighten a little now by taking the plates to the kitchen. Where should I put them?"

Krista liked him even more. "Thanks. On the counter is fine."

He followed her into the kitchen to set down their dishes. Then he followed her to the front door. He paused and said. "Thanks again for bringing Angel home."

"Thank you for the pretty angel ornament."

He nodded. "See you Tuesday."

She smiled at him. "I'll be ready."

The surge of adrenaline from his unexpected visit kept her going for the rest of the afternoon. By dinner time, she was ravenous. She packed the rest of the gingerbread and headed over to see her mom and dad.

The car had gotten chilly. It took several minutes to warm enough to thaw her hands. Though she tried to think about the fun of getting a tree, her thoughts remained on Trent.

A few clouds had moved in, masking the brilliance of the stars. By the time she reached her parents' neighborhood, gentle snowflakes drifted onto the windshield. She turned the wipers on low to brush them away. By the time she reached the house, they had stopped.

She hurried to the door with the gingerbread and her mom greeted her with a hug. "Ooh, you're cold, honey."

"It was snowing a few minutes ago."

"Let's get some warm dinner in you before we get our tree."

Krista set her gingerbread on the kitchen counter and sniffed the oven. "You're making lasagna, aren't you?"

Her mom grinned. "It's your favorite."

Krista sniffed again. The savory scents of tomatoes, garlic, onion, sausage, and meat made her stomach grumble. "Homemade sauce tastes a lot better than the frozen dinners I get when I don't feel like cooking."

Her mom opened the oven to remove the dish. The toasted cheese on top made Krista's mouth water. Rolls and broccoli in a cheese sauce and gingerbread for dessert would follow.

Her dad wandered in. His blue eyes sparkled when he saw her. He gave her a hug. "Baby girl. I'm glad to see you. Your mom went all out on dinner tonight."

Krista laughed. I know."

"What have you been doing?" he asked.

"Mostly working. "

She hesitated. "My neighbor dropped by. I took his little dog home when she got out and he came by to thank me and bring a little gift."

"He?" Her mom's eyebrows shot up.

"Yes. He seems nice. He owns a construction company. He asked me to go to a movie on Tuesday night."

Her dad asked the predictable question. "Do you know him well enough to go with him?"

She knew she'd always be his little girl. "I think so. I'll call you when I get back."

"I'm sure it's fine, George," her mom said. "He still thinks you're sixteen."

"No, Doris. It's a different world than when we were young."

"Yes, dear, but she'll be fine."

"I've wanted to go to a movie. What are you going to see?" George asked.

"George!"

"He doesn't know us," George protested.

Krista told them the movie and time. "I don't care if you come since mom won't let you sit with us."

"Wonderful," her dad said.

"George!"

Krista laughed at her mom's sharp response.

After dinner, they uncovered the gingerbread in the nine by thirteen cakepan.

"It looks like someone got hungry," Doris said.

Sheepish, Krista said, "I shared a little with Trent."

"I guess the rest is mine," George said as he dug into a cakey bite."

"Doris put her hand in his way. "Not so fast. We're dividing it evenly."

They savored the gingerbread with some hot spiced cider and were sated when they left to get the tree.

The lot smelled delightful. Rows of trees stood in proud display while others lay bundled beside the building. From three-foot babies to eight-foot giants, they awaited a Christmas home. Doris and George always chose a six-foot tree that was nice and full. So, Krista concentrated on the size they would want.

She paused beside a tree with full branches and a spicy scent. "This one looks nice."

"It does," Doris agreed.

Krista knew they would buy whatever she suggested. She hoped she'd chosen the best.

"Let's get it," George said.

The attendant carried their choice to the car and helped tie it to the trunk which had been lined with a tarp to catch the wayward needles. When it was secure, they piled into the car for the trip home.

The three of them managed to wrestle it through the front door and into the living room where its stand awaited a new planting. Now, with the tree in place, they began to string the lights and wind golden garland around the branches. The part Krista liked best was putting the ornaments on the tree. Many were handmade and went back two generations. Some of them were ones Krista had made over the years in school. The last thing they added was the shiny tinsel. Now the tree was complete. George took their annual picture in front of the tree to send to the relatives and their work was done. Now came the enjoyment of this beauty until Christmas was over.

"Better get going. It's my week to work Sunday morning at the hospital."

"We'll see you sometime during the week, right?" Doris asked.

Krista smiled at her mom. "You will."

"Tuesday night." George muffled the words in a fake cough.

Doris patted his shoulder. "We'll talk," she assured Krista.

Driving through the still, frigid night, Krista began to second guess Trent's motives for asking her out. What if it was about his gratitude for returning Angel? Maybe, after that, he'd feel he'd paid her back. She shouldn't have gotten so excited about their date.

She sighed. She was tired and having trouble thinking straight. She'd see how she felt in the morning.

CHAPTER THREE

Sunday morning, Jeffrey peered out his bedroom window to see a new snowfall. He marveled at how it sparkled in the sunlight. Before anyone stepped on it, it glistened like millions of diamonds. After being crushed, the beauty disappeared. And it turned brown and ugly.

Mom would want him to shovel the driveway. That was better than having the snow crunched under the car. It got slippery and Mom might fall. Since Mom wasn't up, he put on a warm jacket and got a shovel from the garage.

The morning air was still and cold. Very cold. He blew out a breath of steam and watched it dissipate. He'd learned about that in school, how steam could dissipate. He liked the word and he repeated it in his mind.

He pushed the snow across the driveway and tossed it into the yard. He didn't like the looks of the darkened snow that lay on the edges. However, that couldn't be helped. When the job was almost done, he saw the old man down the block with a snow shovel pushing snow across his driveway. Jeffrey could do it better and faster, so he lifted his shovel and dashed over to help.

The man glanced up in surprise as Jeffrey bounded toward him.

"I can do this real fast. Just watch," Jeffrey said.

The old man leaned on his shovel. He'd been breathing hard and Jeffrey thought it was good for him to take a break.

Jeffrey pushed the snow onto the sides of the yard and tossed it onto the grass as he'd done in his yard. When the old man started to help, Jeffrey repeated, "I can do it. You should go inside and get warm. Then you can come out and see how good it looks when I'm done."

The man Jeffry thought of as a grandpa said, "You're a good kid, son. I am kind of tired. I can pay you something for the job."

Jeffrey shook his head. "I don't want any money. I just want to clear your snow."

The man asked, "Have you had breakfast?"

Jeffrey didn't pause from scooting the snow. "Not yet."

The grandpa said, "When you're finished, ask your mom if you can come in for breakfast. My wife makes a mighty fine one."

That sounded good to Jeffrey. "Okay."

It took him another half hour to finish shoveling. By then Mom had come out to look for him. He saw her and ran home with the shovel.

"I almost got done here but then I saw Grandpa needed help."

Mom gave him a quizzical look. "He's not your grandpa, hon."

"I know, but I like that Grandma and Grandpa better than mine. Mine never come see me."

He hated to talk about them because it made mom look sad, but he had to tell her the truth.

She smoothed back his hair. "They came once when you were born and once when you were a toddler. You don't remember. They would come more, but since they travel overseas a lot, they don't have time."

Jeffrey frowned. "They could come if they wanted to."

He brightened and said, "The grandpa over there said I could eat breakfast with them. Is it okay?"

Lauren glanced down the block. She didn't know the couple, yet she supposed they were probably nice people. She told Jeffrey. "I'll go over with you and meet them. Then, I'll decide."

"I hope you decide yes."

The old man opened the door when Lauren knocked. He smiled broadly and said, "You must be the boy's mother. Come inside. I'm glad to meet you. He's a good kid."

Lauren and Jeffrey stepped into the homey living room. She noticed the cozy sofa covered in a blue and beige afghan. A coffee table covered with magazines sat in front of it and a large leather recliner sat beside the sofa. Best of all, an upright piano filled the wall opposite the sofa. Lauren loved the sound of a piano. Her mother had played well and insisted Lauren take lessons. She had complied until she reached her teens and then stopped playing. She'd hardly touched one in years.

An elderly woman appeared in the doorway at the end of the living room. Lauren supposed it opened to the kitchen if they had a similar floor plan.

The woman's smile was hesitant, yet her words were warm. "Vic told me you might be joining us. I'm Abby and you're very welcome to eat with us."

"You really don't have to do this. You didn't expect our company," Lauren said.

"I've already added extra bacon and eggs. It's more than we can eat. If you don't stay it will go to waste. You and your son are both welcome."

"She makes a great Sunday breakfast. Wait until you taste her biscuits," the grandpa added.

"Then we'd love to stay. It's very generous of you to have us."

The grandpa laid a hand on Jeffrey's shoulder. Lauren was surprised when her son didn't flinch away.

"You should have seen how hard this boy worked," the man said. "He deserves a good meal."

He shovels our driveway, too," Lauren said. "It's just something he likes to do."

"It saved me a lot of work. I'm not as young as I used to be," Grandpa admitted.

"Come sit before the food gets cold," Grandma said.

They went obediently into the kitchen to see a huge spread of bacon and eggs, biscuits with honey butter, and jelly, a carafe of coffee and pitcher of milk all set on the table. Cheerful blue country Dutch plates completed the homey feel of the house.

"This looks so good," Lauren said. The scents were making her stomach rumble.

"Let's sit down, then," Grandma shooed them into chairs.

The food tasted every bit as good as it looked. Jeffrey polished off more than Lauren had ever seen him eat in a meal. She could still taste the honey butter on her tongue when they finished the meal. "This was a real treat. We usually have cereal or toast on Sunday morning."

"I'm glad you enjoyed it," Grandma said.

"I want to come every week," Jeffrey said.

Heat rose to Lauren's cheeks. "You can't come every week, son. This is a lot of work for your friends."

"Nonsense. You are both welcome," Grandma said. "I love cooking for folks and I hardly ever get to do it. None of our family lives in town. You come next week, and I'll open a jar of my fresh peach preserves for the biscuits," Grandma said.

"It sounds heavenly," Lauren admitted. "Let me help you with the dishes before we go."

"That's sweet of you, honey," Grandma said.

As they got up to help, Grandpa asked. "Do you and the boy have a church you're attending?"

"No. It's been a while since we've been. Jeffrey doesn't always do well in social situations."

"I bet he'd do fine at our church. He could go to Sunday school while we're in church. The kids love it. Would you like to try?"

"Please, Mom. I want to go," Jeffrey begged.

Lauren wished now they'd not come over. "Jeffrey, the Sunday school teachers won't know what to do if you get angry."

Jeffrey shook his head. His eyes pleaded with her. "I won't get mad. I promise."

"You'll never know if you don't let him try," Grandpa said.

Lauren turned to Jeffrey. "You can't hurt anyone."

"I won't."

Lauren had never seen him so sincere. "All right. We'll try. We have to change clothes."

"You're fine like you are. We aren't' a fancy church," Grandpa said. "Can you be ready in fifteen minutes?"

"I'm ready now," Jeffrey said.

Lauren hadn't seen him like this in years. "Let's go home and brush our hair and teeth. Then we'll come back," Lauren said.

Grandpa walked them to the door. "We're sure happy to have you."

"I hope it goes well," Lauren said.

"It will," he assured her.

He didn't know the possibility of Jeffrey's temper.

A few minutes later, Laruen and Jeffrey returned. They rode together in the elderly couples' car. Sunday traffic was light on this snow-blown day, and they reached the church in less than ten minutes.

It was a simple brownstone building that sprawled across a half-acre of property with plenty of room for parking. Lauren's palms grew sweaty when Grandpa turned off the car to go inside. This would either be wonderful or a total disaster.

Two friendly gentlemen opened the doors and welcomed them in. "I see you brought guests," one said. "Is this your family?"

These are our neighbors," Grandpa answered. This young man shoveled my driveway this morning."

"What a nice young man." The gentleman reached out for Jeffrey's hand and Jeffrey shook with him, amazing Lauren.

Inside, the church was cozy and warm. A large Christmas tree trimmed with angels and doves sat to the side of the double doors leading into the sanctuary. The scene brought tears to Lauren's eyes. It had been a long time since she'd been to church. Jeffrey's father was an avowed atheist who refused to go and now had nothing to do with them. Although the few times she'd gone with friends had inspired her, she wasn't brave enough to go on her own.

While Grandma chatted with parishioners, Lauren and Jeffrey followed Grandpa down a hallway with open doors on either side. They stopped in front of one labeled fourth to fifth grade.

"What grade are you in?" grandpa asked Jeffrey.

"Fifth."

"Then here you are," Grandpa said.

A man Lauren's age came to the door to greet them. "Is this your grandson, Vic?"

"No. But I'd be proud to say he was. He's a friend."

The man looked into Jeffrey's eyes and said, "We are glad to have you here today. Come in and join us. We're all friends here."

Jeffrey went in without a look back. He could be bold. Too bold sometimes, Lauren thought.

"Be good, Jeffrey," Lauren reminded him. She knew he wasn't listening.

The sanctuary was beautifully decorated with gold and silver garlands draped down the pews. Artificial poinsettia leaves were fastened at each end and the altar held potted poinsettias in beautiful red blooms. The service began with prayer, and then Christmas hymns that Lauren hadn't sung in a long time.

During the sermon, the pastor talked about the meaning and magnitude of Christmas. For so long, Lauren had been caught up in the extra stress of her job during December and the business of shopping that she hadn't thought much about the true meaning of Christmas. Since her parents weren't church-goers, Lauren had only been to church services a couple of times in her life. Perhaps that was why the sermon gave her a lot to think about.

After the closing hymn, they greeted people as they walked down the hallway to Jeffrey's class. Lauren tensed as they reached the doorway. No one had come to get her from church, so maybe Jeffrey had been okay. Still, she wondered what she was going to hear from the teacher.

Looking over the half door to the classroom she saw the kids at a table, fully engaged by the lesson. They were playing a game in which the teacher asked, "For the last question, who led the Israelites to the Promised Land?"

A chorus of voices shouted, "Moses!"

"Right," he said. "For that answer everyone gets a coupon for a free scoop of ice cream at Mr. Miller's Shop. If you don't know where it is, the address is on the coupon."

Jeffrey jumped up with the other kids and shouted, "Yes."

Lauren went weak with relief. She swallowed over a lump in her throat to see him so happily engaged. "He did it," she told her elderly companions.

"Of course he did," Grandpa replied.

On the way home, Jeffrey talked about the fun he'd had and all he'd learned. "We can get the ice cream, right?"

Lauren was so pleased he'd done well, she said, "We'll go after lunch."

"Yes!"

"We're happy you enjoyed your class," Grandma said.

"I want to go back," Jeffrey said. "Can I, Mom?"

Pressure rose in Lauren's chest at the thought of going alone with Jeffrey to the church. "I don't know. We'll see."

"That's what you say when we don't do things," he fumed.

"You're always welcome to go with us," Grandpa said.

"That would be great," Lauren said. "Thank you."

Now, she wouldn't have to go alone.

"That makes us happy," Grandma said. "Our kids live so far away that we don't get to do much with them."

"But we're right here," Jeffrey said.

For the first time in a long time, he looked totally happy. Lauren hoped it would last.

CHAPTER FOUR

Trent couldn't get Krista out of his mind. He had first seen her a few times leaving her house and again on the porch of the elderly couple. Though he'd admired her, he couldn't think of a way to introduce himself. Then Angel had provided him an opportunity. He'd rewarded her with an extra treat that night, even though she had managed an unauthorized escape.

It was hard to concentrate on work on Tuesday afternoon. He kept thinking of Krista and her sweet smile. She was pretty. More importantly, she showed a wet and gentle spirit, and she liked his dog.

When he got off work, he went home for a quick shower and shave. He'd picked up a small potted poinsettia at the store and now hoped he hadn't made a mistake. Not all women liked flowers.

He parked in front of her red brick one story with crisp white trim. He strode up the sidewalk to the porch and rang the bell. By the end of the evening, he hoped to know much more about her.

She opened the door and smiled, then drew a quick breath when she saw the plant.

"How pretty."

He held it out to her. "I hope you like plants. I don't have any because I have no idea how to take care of them. If you don't care for them, I can take it back.'

"No, I love it," she assured him. My mom has all sorts of plants that I take care of when she goes out of town, which isn't too often. Still I've learned the basics of what to do with them."

He studied the red blooms at the end if the branches.

"They had white ones too, but I liked the red."

She smiled again." Me, too. Step inside while I set it on the coffee table."

Trent stepped into the foyer and shut the door against the chilly evening. He watched her graceful movement as she swept into the living room and deposited the plant on the wooden coffee table where they had eaten gingerbread. They had sat on her sofa and he had become infatuated with her.

They walked to the car and Trent opened her door and watched her slide inside. She pulled her calf-length sapphire skirt in with her. It rippled gracefully like a wave coming in from the sea. When they were both buckled, he started the car and drove out of the cul-de-sac onto the main road through the subdivision.

Trent turned on Main Street and headed toward the theater. With only a week until Christmas, the city had strung garlands with big red bows between the light poles. The stores had twinkling Christmas lights glowing around their windows and pedestrians carried boxes and bags as they strode along the sidewalk. The sights and smells of Christmas always brought Trent back to childhood. It had been such fun then.

He turned to Krista. "What's your favorite holiday? Christmas, Thanksgiving? Easter?"

She thought a moment. "I think it's Christmas. Our family traditions go way back besides the fact that it's a sacred time. What about you?"

"When I was a kid, I would have said Christmas. Now it's Thanksgiving. My brother comes down and stays with my mom. We all have dinner together."

"You're lucky. I don't have siblings."

He chuckled. "When I was a kid, I wouldn't have agreed it was lucky and neither would my brother. We fought at least once a day."

Krista cocked her head. "From what I've heard, that's normal."

He grinned. "I suppose so."

At the theater, Trent bought the sodas and they settled into the middle section of seats. On this Tuesday night so close to Christmas, it wasn't crowded. Perhaps everyone was Christmas shopping. Sitting close to Krista allowed him to enjoy the lavender scent of her hair. He couldn't believe his fortune to have met this lovely woman who lived only yards from his house.

Krista took a sip of her drink and smiled at him. "This is a rare treat. I don't keep sodas around the house."

Her lips were tinted slightly redder from the beverage. He drew his gaze away. "I keep a fridge pack of my favorite and try not to go through them too fast."

The previews started and they settled in, shoulders touching, to wait for the movie.

If Krista liked action, that was what she got. The hero fought constant peril in order to save a secret government site and its workers from falling into enemy hands. His nearly fatal ending had them glued to the screen. When he overcame all odds and saved the day with the arrival of support, they sat back in their seats and took deep breaths.

"That was really good," Krista said.

"The kind you like?" Trent asked.

"Oh, yes. Not boring at all."

"I'd say it was adrenaline pumping action," Trent added.

"Exactly."

Outside, the clouds had cleared to reveal the brightest stars that forced their light through the interference of the streetlights. Krista gazed up at the sky, so cold and clear. I love nights like this. Everything is still and quiet. It's like the world is under a spell of peace and calmness."

"It will be someday. Do you believe in God?"

Still staring at the sky, Krista said, "Yes. I do. How else would all this exist."

Trent wanted to kiss her on the cheek. He resisted the urge. It was too soon and not worth the risk of offending her. Instead, he took her arm as they headed to the car.

"Would you like to stop for coffee and warm up?" He asked.

"I would love a hot cup. Just holding it in my hands sounds good right now."

He grinned. "Maybe I'll get two for you, one to hold and one to drink."

Her sweet laughter rang in the night. "That's okay. One is enough for both jobs."

He helped her into the car and drove to the nearby diner. It was known for its exceptional pie and coffee.

Inside, it was as brightly lit as the theater had been dim. They sat at a booth with a gleaming Formica tabletop and waited until a middle-aged waitress with gray hair and round glasses come over to greet them and take their order.

She repeated, "Two coffees with cream."

Then she asked, "We have some tempting pies. Apple, Cherry, Peach, and Pecan. May I get you some?"

Trent noticed her vivid blue eyes behind the glasses and thought she must have been quite beautiful in her youth. Krista would be like that. She would still be attractive in middle-age.

He told Krista, "I'd like a slice of peach pie. What about you? Want to join me?"

She smiled. "Yes, only I would like cherry, please."

The waitress nodded and promised to have it right out.

"She's nice." Krista said.

"Yes, she is. It's great when people don't lose their Christmas spirit this time of year."

Krista nodded. "That's why I don't wait to shop until right before Christmas. It's too easy to get caught up in the rush and stress."

"Tell me more about your family," Trent said. "Who's on your shopping list?"

"Not too many, just my Mom, Dad, Grandma and a couple of people at work. How about you?" Krista asked.

"I have my mom and brother, and I send a gift card to my aunt and uncle. I don't know what they'd like for gifts"

"I'm sure they like cards. Who doesn't? My Grandmother loves flowers, so that's easy to shop for her. My parents are harder."

Krista's gaze turned quizzical. "You know I'm a nurse. I don't know anything about your job. What do you do?"

A touch of a smile lifted the corners of his mouth. "It's nothing exciting. I'm a business contractor. I have three office employees and my crew of laborers."

'You're a business owner. That's a lot of responsibility. My mom works at Whitewater Bank and Trust. I wonder if they carry your loan."

"That would be the one. I guess she could look up my records."

She hesitated. She could if you want her to."

"That's okay. We're current on the loan."

She studied him a moment. "She wouldn't spy on you."

He gave her an apologetic smile. "I know. I trust you and your mother."

He hoped he hadn't offended her. It had been a knee-jerk reaction to protect his privacy. There was too much spying going on with personal information. Still, he shouldn't have cast suspicion on Krista's mom.

They changed topics and spoke about their childhoods and teen years. Trent said, "I'd never planned to be a contractor. I studied architecture in college. Then, my brother started building business structures and houses here in town. When he decided to move away, I bought him out. I'm glad I did. I really enjoy it."

Krista finished her coffee and set down the mug. "It's good to love what you do. I enjoy nursing but it's not a passion."

Trent thought about her comment and asked, "What would you do if you had a choice of anything?"

She answered quickly. "I'd teach ballet. I took lessons all the way through high school and even into college. I can't make enough money working as an assistant in a studio."

Trent had noticed how gracefully she moved when they first met. Now he knew why. Without intent, he immediately began to plan her studio in his mind.

He pulled his thoughts back to her comments. "Have you ever thought about financing a studio? You could rent a building and teach part-time to make payments."

"I could only teach after six-thirty on weekdays and Saturdays. I don't think I'd have enough kids sign up and certainly not enough adults since I'd be competing with the other dance academy in town."

"Maybe they'd work with you as a branch."

She thought about it. "I don't know. The owner who taught me sold out and retired. I haven't met the new owner. She would have to make enough to pay rent on another building and pay me. I don't believe I'd make any more than if I worked in her studio."

Trent understood her problem. Opening a business was expensive and would eat a lot of her salary. To grow it, she would have to hire teachers and that would cost even more.

She smiled at him. "You don't have to figure it out. I'm happy where I am."

"Was it that obvious that I was trying to solve it?"

Her grin melted his heart. "Yes."

They had finished the pie and coffee and Trent knew he should take her home. They both had work in the morning. Yet, he didn't want to part with her. She solved his dilemma by saying," I should get home. A couple of us have a meeting with a supervisor first thing in the morning."

He regretted that she was right. They should get home.

He said, "I need to get back, too."

He paid the tab and they walked out to the sound of the door jingling behind them, another reminder that Christmas was near. Lit street decorations gave confirmation.

The still air captured their breath in frosty puffs of smoke. When they got into the car, Trent cranked up the heater to warm their numb appendages.

As they drove through their neighborhood, Krista commented on the decorated houses and yards. "I love the lights and manger scenes and the reindeer and candy canes. Yards are so pretty all lit up. Even though I don't do any of that, I like to look."

When Trent agreed, an idea came to mind.

"Do you have time this week to drive around and look at the lights in other parts of the city?"

She didn't hesitate to say, "I'd love to. I have Friday night free."

"Friday it is. If you can go to dinner first, we could eat at six-thirty and then look at lights."

"I can. It sounds really fun."

He parked in her driveway and walked her to her door. She turned to him and said, "I had a wonderful time."

"So did I." His pulse quickened. Would she wait for a kiss?

She reached into her purse for her key and put it into the lock. "I'll see you Friday."

"I'm looking forward to it."

Even though he didn't get to kiss her, his elation to have another date kept disappointment at bay. Besides, Friday would offer another chance.

CHAPTER FIVE

Lauren dropped Jeffrey off with the only sitter who would still take him while Lauren was at work. He'd been expelled from a kid's club and two daycare centers because of disruptive behavior. She often wondered if anyone knew how hard it was to be a single mom with a special needs child. Instead of sympathy and support, she often endured criticism and disapproval. She'd cried herself to sleep on countless nights due to one incident or another.

He hadn't wanted to go, arguing he was old enough to be home alone. It took bribery to get him to stop dragging his feet and get into the car. She'd be late to work unless she pushed the speed limit.

When she pulled into a parking space at the office supply store where she did bookwork, she fervently hoped she wouldn't get a call from the sitter. She used her key code and stepped into the store. She enjoyed the scent of paper and ink. It reminded her of the crisp smell of clothes from the dryer. Toward the back of the store, she passed the office furniture. She spun one of the desk chairs in a circle on her way past.

When she settled at her desk in her office cubby, she turned on the computer. As she centered her mind on the work ahead of her, her boss popped into the room. Their relationship was good, and Carol had been understanding about Lauren's family difficulties.

"How are you holding up during Jeffrey's school break?" Carol asked.

Lauren smiled at the middle-aged woman whose gray eyes peered behind round glasses that made her look owlish.

"So far, so good. He didn't want to go to the sitter's house today, so I bribed him."

Carol nodded. "I say to do whatever works. Why doesn't he like her?"

"I don't think it's that. He gets bored playing video games and watching television all day. I can't allow him to go outside because I worry he might leave."

"I see the problem," Carol said. "You'll be glad when he's back in school."

Lauren nodded. "I sure will."

They talked business for a few minutes before Carol said," Don't forget the Christmas party on Saturday night. We are giving away some good gifts in our drawing and making an announcement you'll want to hear."

Lauren drew a deep breath to release the pressure that made her stiffen until her bones hurt. This meant asking the sitter to watch Jeffrey again as well as more money spent on an already tight budget.

"I'll try, but I'll have to check with the sitter."

I'm sure you can find someone to watch him. The party is only once a year. I don't want you to miss it."

Carol sounded empathetic. Nonetheless, the pressure inside Lauren edged up a notch. "I'll really try," she promised.

Even Carol didn't truly realize the difficulty of her situation. For the hundredth time, she felt all alone at this festive time of year. At least, today, she could bury herself in her work and forget her other obligations.

She worked through lunchtime so that she could leave early to pick up the new game Jeffrey wanted for Christmas for his computer. Limiting his time on his games was difficult. She would have tried harder except for the fact that his pastime gave her a much-needed break.

She closed the office at four-thirty and told Carol she'd finished for the day. "I'm going by to get a computer game for Jeffrey. He wants that and something called a switch for Christmas. I think it's an update that he downloads, but I'm not sure."

Carol shook her head. "He's smarter than I am. I can do my personal finances and e-mail and that's about it."

"I hope that gives me job security," Lauren said.

Carol gave her a wink. "You bet."

Lauren drove to the store through crowded streets that made changing lanes difficult. Finding a parking space took two trips through the lot. As expected, the largest electronics store in town was crowded with Christmas shoppers. Announcements about sales blared over the loudspeakers and the lines grew longer at each register. Lauren described what she wanted to a harried young sales associate. He led her around a corner to an aisle where the video games were located.

"What game system does he have?"

Carol looked at her notes she'd scribbled when Jeffrey told her about the game. She told the clerk and he quickly dug it out.

After fifteen minutes in the checkout line, she was finally on her way home.

At the light at Franklin Street, Lauren's car sputtered and rolled to a stop. She tried restarting it, with no luck. Her heart thumped wildly as she ground the starter. A clicking sound met her efforts. She turned on her hazard lights as the car behind her angrily honked.

She tried again and the clicking was all she got. Dead battery. She had just grabbed her phone to try finding a tow when a middle-aged gentleman stood at her window.

She rolled it down and he said," I see you're stalled. Do you need help?"

She took a breath to steady her voice. "My battery is dead. I'm looking for a tow."

"If it's your battery, let's get you out of the way and I can give you a jump."

Her chest flooded with relief. "Thank you. I feel terrible blocking this lane."

"I'm the only one behind you now. Everyone else is going around. Put your car in neutral and I'll give you a push when the light turns green. We can park on the side street to jump your car."

"Thank you so much."

Lauren wiped her clammy hands on her slacks as the man walked away and got into his car. She put her car in neutral and waited for the light.

When it turned green, she felt his car tap gently against her bumper, and she began to move. They crossed two lanes of traffic and continued to the side street where the stranger in a heavy tweed coat parked facing the front of her car.

When she got out, he said, "Stay in the car where it's warm. All you need to do is start your car when I give you the signal."

She waited while he hooked up his cables and started his car. When he gave her the signal with a thumbs-up, she turned the key. Hearing it sputter to life was the best thing she'd heard all day. She grabbed her wallet and hurried out to him as he got out to unhook his cables.

"May I give you something for your trouble?" She asked.

"Absolutely not. We're put on this earth to help each other. Will you be okay to get a new battery?"

"Yes. I'm going to the store right now."

"Don't turn your car off until you get there."

She already knew this, yet didn't mind hearing it from this kind, blue-eyed stranger.

"God bless," he said, as he walked away.

"You, too," she called out.

When she reached the auto parts of the large discount store, she hurried in to buy a battery and to get it installed. The unexpected expense would hurt her pocketbook and cut into her meager savings. However, it couldn't be helped.

A young clerk looked-up her information from the last time she'd had a battery replaced. "It's been six years," he said. "I'm afraid it's no longer under warranty."

She knew it wouldn't be. "Will you be able to do it tonight?"

"Yes. There's about a two- hour wait."

Lauren signed. There was really nothing else she could do.

She called Ruby, the sitter, and explained what had happened.

"Oh dear," Ruby said. "I was planning on going out with a couple of friends to look at Christmas lights. I'll have to see if they can do it a little later. It'll cost you extra."

"I know, but I really am stuck. I'm so sorry."

Ruby signed loudly. "These things happen even when they're not convenient."

"I'm so sorry, Ruby."

She heard a longer sigh, and, after a pause, Ruby said, "It's all right."

Lauren hadn't dared ask Ruby about sitting for her on Saturday night. She'd wait until she got there to see if she was agreeable. If not, what would she do?

It took a little past two hours for the car to be finished. After she paid the bill, Lauren hurried to Ruby's house. The fact that she'd inconvenienced Ruby made her uneasy.

She arrived just after eight o'clock. When Ruby opened the door, Lauren apologized again. "We'll hurry off. I hope you can still look at the lights."

Ruby sighed. "My friends are coming by as soon as I give them a call."

"Good. How much do I owe you?"

She paid Ruby the extra charge and called for Jeffrey.

He approached from the living room. He was frowning. "You're late."

"I couldn't help it, honey. My battery died and I had to get it fixed."

"I hate it when you're late," he grumbled.

"I'm sorry, honey." She knew it would be hard to appease him. Waiting was hard for Jeffrey. He had very little patience.

"He had a snack, but not a real supper," Ruby said. "I was expecting you to come in time to feed him."

"I hope I gave you enough to cover the snack," Lauren said.

Ruby nodded. "I added it to your charge."

Lauren's muscles tensed as she asked, "Would you be able to watch Jeffrey on Saturday evening?"

Jeffrey groaned and Lauren felt her cheeks flush with embarrassment. She ignored her son and waited for Ruby's answer.

"I'm sorry Mrs. Baker, I can't watch him on Saturday. I've got plans."

She fidgeted and Lauren knew Ruby was impatient for them to leave. Whatever was she going to do now? Carol had made it clear that she wanted Lauren to attend the Christmas party. How was she going to find a new sitter so quickly?

Jeffrey tugged at her coat. "Let's go, Mom."

She followed him out the door into the chill of velvet darkness that enveloped the neighborhood. The stillness allowed the sound of carolers singing "Silent Night" to drift to her ears. She stared into the sky and wondered what it would have been like to see angels appear. Had it really happened, or was it a lovely myth? When life got hard it would be nice to believe there was something more, something greater in store. Could she really believe this?

Once they were both buckled in the car, Jeffrey asked, Then, he asked, "Can we stop and get burgers? I'm hungry. Ruby was mean. She gave me an apple and a pack of crackers. When I said I was still hungry, she said I could wait till you got there."

"It was nice of her to feed you at all. I didn't realize she had plans for the evening."

Jeffrey snorted. "It wasn't real plans. She wasn't going to the moon or anything. She was just going light-looking with her friends who are probably as mean as she is."

Lauren ignored his assessment of Ruby's friends. "I have hoagie fixings in the fridge for us tonight. We can have chips and dip with it."

She braced herself for his complaint.

Sure enough, he said, "I don't feel like hoagies. I want something hot, like a hamburger and fries."

She explained often that they couldn't afford fast food very frequently. Nor did she think it was good for him. Instead of repeating herself, she said, "We'll turn on a movie and eat in the living room. You can stay up a little later tonight."

"Hey, can I have some soda, too?"

"A little." Lauren had not been able to decide if sugar made his behavior worse. Yet tonight she needed him to be calm. She was stressed about what to do with him on Saturday night. Most kids his age would have friends with parents she could call. Jeffrey didn't have friends. Other boys his age were scared of him and his temper. They avoided him during the portion of the day when his special needs class was mainstreamed with the other students.

She watched him as he chuckled at the antics of the Grinch. Right then, Jeffrey looked every bit a normal ten-year-old boy. Yet his metamorphosis into Mr. Hyde could leave a wake of smashed objects on the floor. It hadn't happened in the last two weeks, which was encouraging. However, Lauren knew that anger lurked inside him, waiting to come out. More than one Christmas had been ruined when he either didn't get the toy he wanted, or he broke what he did get soon after opening it.

She sighed, longing for the perfect Christmas photo moment to place in the album on her phone. Maybe this year would be one she would want to remember.

When the movie ended and she bribed him into bed with a promise to make pancakes in the morning, she sat in the dimly lit living room and stared at the corner where Jeffrey would want to put a tree. The living room was not large enough to hold a towering pine like the one he liked in the mall. They usually got a four-foot tree and shoved the sofa and coffee table towards the entryway to make room. The leather armchair she'd found at a garage sale had to be moved from beside the sofa to a spot in front of the fireplace, leaving a narrow walkway between the chair and sofa.

The wall-mounted television with movie storage beneath it took up the far wall, and the roll-top desk she had inherited from her grandfather stayed on the wall near the archway to the kitchen. Since there wasn't an additional family room, the tree crowded their space. Lauren reminded herself that it was only once a year and that if she became a Grinch it wouldn't do anyone any good. The tree would be up for a week and then the removing of ornaments and packing them away would be behind her. She would do it because it made Jeffrey happy. One day, he would grow up, for better or worse, and he would be on his own. Hopefully, she would miss Jeffrey and the need for a tree.

Saturday morning dawned cold with thick gray clouds that swirled across the sky and she was reminded of her only attempt to make homemade gravy that had lumped in the pan into gray globs.

After Jeffrey pulled himself out of bed and downed a bowl of cereal, she told him, "We need to run by the store."

He usually balked. Today he said, "Good. I need some more paint. I'm doing a painting of Grandma and Grandpa's house and I ran out of brown and white. I want to finish it as a Christmas present for them. They've been nice to me. Grandpa plays chess and checkers with me and Grandma makes me cookies."

She stared in amazement. He'd never crafted a present for anyone except her. His relationship with them gave her hope that he might learn to relate to and care about others.

"That's wonderful, honey. Of course, we'll get your paint."

He beamed. "We'll need a frame, too, so they can put it on the wall."

Her heart lurched. If they didn't hang his work he would be devastated. The elderly couple had invited them to Sunday breakfast. If she and Jeffrey came, Jeffrey would notice if his work was not displayed. A meltdown would likely follow. Yet she could hardly tell Abby and Vic they had to hang a painting done by a child among their beautiful originals collected as mementos of trips across the country. Almost all their collection was of towering mountains and rustic forests done in a realistic style.

He studied her, a slight frown forming on his face. 'We'll get a frame, too, won't we? It's not a real present until it's framed."

Lauren smiled at her son. Her heart ached for him and his problems. "We'll get a frame, the best we can afford."

Jeffrey smiled back. The anxiety was gone from his face. Sometimes it took very little to make him happy. Other times, it was impossible. If only he could always be this sweet.

"Measure your painting so we know what size frame to get," she told Jeffrey.

He ran to his room to use his ruler and returned to say, "Eight and a half by eleven inches. I measured twice to be sure."

"Good," Lauren said. "That's a common frame size. We should be able to find one easily."

The store was crowded on Saturday morning. A lot of folks were buying the fixings for Christmas dinner in two weeks. Lauren wished for the hundredth time that her parents were close, and they could celebrate as they'd done when she was a child. They weren't, and she needed to accept it. One thing she'd learned too late was that she could never return to the past and appreciate what she'd had then. There was only the present and the future.

They'd picked out the necessities and a frozen cherry pie as a treat for Christmas Day. After they checked out the groceries, Lauren said, "We'll get your frame now. You can't take too long. Even though it's cold outside, some of the frozen food might start to melt in the car."

"Can we get a tree tonight?" Jeffrey asked.

Anxiety tightened Lauren's breathing. "I don't know. I'm supposed to go to a Christmas party at work and I haven't found anyone to stay with you."

Jeffrey frowned. "I bet the party's stupid. We should get a tree instead."

"The people I work for really want me to come, but we'll see. When we get back I'm going to make a couple of phone calls to see if anyone can watch you tonight."

Jeffrey didn't reply. He didn't even seem to be listening. Then he said, "I want a goose for Christmas dinner. That's what they have in England. I know because we've been studying it in class. The English people stuff it and bake it and eat it along with fresh cranberries and they have a special pudding for dessert. Sometimes they have eel. We could try that, too."

Lauren shook her head. "We're sticking with turkey."

"Okay, but you won't know what the other stuff tastes like."

They headed to the craft store. Traffic crowded the city streets. Lauren cringed at the sound of horns as drivers switched lanes unexpectedly. People were so hurried at Christmas, more than any other time of year, and many of them got into very bad moods very fast. She was relieved once they parked at the store and Jeffrey picked out a frame. It didn't take him long to choose a light oak one that was on sale. He held his treasure while they waited in line and finally checked out. Lauren felt exhausted and still had to call around to see if she could find a sitter.

As they neared their house and turned the corner to their cul-de-sac, Jeffrey suddenly shouted for her to stop. Lauren stomped on the brake, sure that she'd nearly hit a pet when Jeffrey hopped from the car and scurried toward his adopted Grandma. She paused in her driveway and heard his voice.

"Hi, Grandma Abby." His eyes shone. "Mom can't find anyone to watch me tonight. May I stay with you and Grandpa?"

Abby's eyes locked with Lauren's as Lauren felt her cheeks heat with embarrassment. Did Grandma Abby think Lauren had set him up to do this? She hurried to explain. "I'm so sorry. I'm afraid this is his idea. I have a party at work tonight and his regular sitter couldn't watch him. I'm making some calls this afternoon to try to find someone."

Abby smiled at Jeffrey. "Of course he may stay with us this evening. We'd love some company."

Jeffrey threw his arms up in excitement. "Grandpa said he'd teach me how to play checkers and chess."

Abby's grin widened. "I'm sure he will. He's missed you all week."

"Really?" Jeffrey beamed with delight.

"Yes, really."

Grandma Abby asked Lauren, "What time do you need to leave, dear?"

"About six-fifteen. It starts at six-thirty."

"Send Jeffrey over for supper at six and then you can go whenever you're ready."

Lauren's eyes welled with tears. "You've no idea how grateful I am."

Grandma Abby chuckled. "I probably do. We enjoy Jeffrey's company. You go have fun."

Grandma Abby went inside, and Lauren and Jeffrey continued home. Jeffrey was beaming. "I told you they'd want me, Mom."

"You were right." Lauren remained amazed at how taken Jeffrey was with this elderly couple. They appeared to genuinely enjoy him, too. God must have brought them together. Abby insisted that things didn't happen without a reason.

Jeffrey worked on the painting for two hours and let it dry so that he could frame it. When he dragged her in to admire it, she had to admit it had turned out nicely. He had sketched out their chocolate brown house with white trim and tall maple trees, one on each side of the front yard. The sidewalk up to the house curved from the front sidewalk to the two-step concrete porch. He had drawn the large picture window on the right side of the house with a smaller window on the left. The picture window showed a brightly lit Christmas tree inside. The tree had blue and red balls and a golden star on top. On the bottom right corner, Jeffrey had signed it, "With Love, From Jeffrey."

"I don't want them to ever forget me," he said.

Lauren gave him a gentle hug and was pleased when he didn't pull away. "They won't forget you," she said.

CHAPTER SIX

Grandma Abby was waiting for Jeffrey when Lauren dropped him off. "Guess what's for supper?" she said.

Jeffrey said, "Pizza?"

"Nope. I made my grandma's fried chicken recipe with mashed potatoes and gravy."

"Wow. We never have that, do we Mom?" he asked Lauren.

"Nope. I don't know how to make it so that it tastes the way you like."

"I bet I'll like this," Jeffrey said.

"You will," Grandma Abby assured him.

She smiled at Lauren. "You go on and have a good time. We'll be fine here. After supper, Grandpa has a game of checkers set up for him and Jeffrey."

"Play nicely," Lauren warned Jeffrey.

"I will, Mom."

Lauren didn't hug him because she didn't know if he'd like it. "

Instead, she said, "Have fun."

"I will." He was already headed toward the kitchen. She heard him telling Grandma Mandy that he'd made a present for them.

It seemed her problem had solved itself. Jeffrey was where he most wanted to be and now Lauren could go to Carol's party. Grandma Abby would say it was the hand of God. Lauren was beginning to think she was right.

The office party was just beginning when she arrived. The usual jingle of the bell atop the door sounded more festive with a lit tree at the entrance. A silver garland encircled the branches and ornaments of blue, red, and gold glowed in the lights. Under the tree, at least a dozen presents lay wrapped in shiny foil paper. The cares that wore at her lifted as she was reminded of her childhood of sugar cookies and school Christmas parties. Back in those days, her worst fear had been forgetting her homework.

In the space between the checkout stands and the island, a full table was laid out with enchiladas labeled either red or green. Toppings in bowls decorated with red and green chilies sat next to the main dish. Tortilla chips and lettuce salad sat in large bowls. She breathed the spicy scent and her stomach rumbled.

Carol hustled to greet her. "Hang your coat in the back. We're just getting ready to eat. There are juice, punch, and tea, as well as desserts on the other table."

She pointed to a table that sat crossways to the enchilada one.

"I don't want any left-over's," she added.

Lauren hung her coat on a hook behind her office door and returned to the party. A half-dozen cashiers, copy clerks, and the stockers sat in folding chairs in a circle near the food. Lauren took a seat beside Eleanor, one of the middle-aged checkers and waited for Carol to tell them what was next.

"Get a drink, Lauren," Carol said. "Everyone must have a drink of some sort so that we can have a toast."

Lauren did as ordered and returned with a glass of tea. They lifted their glasses and Carol toasted "To the best staff anyone could ask to have and to your health, happiness, and finances as we come near to entering a new year."

Everyone repeated the words before clinking glasses with a neighbor and with Carol who came to each of them.

"She really is an amazing boss," Lauren thought.

"Now we eat," Carol said.

Everyone cheered as they crowded the table to load up on enchiladas. Lauren plopped two plump green ones onto her plate, and she added salad on the side. When everyone had food, they took their chairs to the table to eat. One bite told Carol whoever made these enchiladas knew what she was doing. They were a perfection of spice, meat, and sauce. She'd not eaten much lunch and the flavor delighted her tongue.

Carol sat on one side of Lauren and a sweet checker named Beth sat on the other. Lauren turned to Carol. These are amazing enchiladas. Who made them?"

"Turn to the right and you'll see her."

"Beth, you made these? They're amazing."

Beth beamed. Her dark eyes sparkled. Her round jovial face reminded Lauren of Mrs. Claus and Lauren could imagine her in the kitchen cooking for Santa.

"I made plenty so everybody can take some home."

"My son will love them. Thank you.

Lauren would enjoy not having to cook.

"It's just you and your son, right?" Beth asked.

"Yes. The older he gets the more his appetite grows. He's ten and can eat almost a whole pizza. I won't be able to afford him by the time he's a teenager," Lauren said.

Beth chuckled. "I have two teen-aged boys and they go through three gallons of milk a week."

"Wow. We only go through one and I thought that was bad," Lauren said.

Beth nodded knowingly. "Just wait."

"I'm glad you found a sitter and could come tonight," Carol told Lauren.

Lauren savored a bite of enchilada, and then said, "Jeffrey adores the older couple who live on our block. They invited him over for dinner and games."

"You're lucky. Not all older people have the patience to have kids around," Carol said. "Do your parents see him much?"

The pang of loneliness Lauren always felt when she thought about her parents shot through her. "No. They live a long way off and travel a lot. We almost never see them."

"Too bad. At least you have your neighbors," Carol said.

They chatted about Christmas plans and relatives while everyone finished their meal. For dessert, Lauren delved into decadent dark fudge. She savored the taste on her tongue, wanting it to last as long as possible. She finally followed it with a turtle cookie topped with caramel and pecan. She forced herself to stop or she'd never be able to sleep tonight.

Carol rang the beautiful silver bell that decorated the middle of the table. Everyone gave her their attention. "I would like each of you to bring your chair over near the Christmas tree and form a circle "

Everyone did as she asked.

"I have a present for each of you," Carol said.

Memories of being a child on Christmas morning made Lauren smile. Her parents had told her that adults loved Christmas as much as kids. Her mom had always sent small presents to the grandparents, aunts, and uncles. It was a challenge and a joy for her to pick them out. Judging by the notes she got, they greatly appreciated her remembering them.

"You can't open yours until everyone has a present," Carol said.

Her eyes sparkled showing her pleasure at being a good and gracious hostess. Lauren swallowed over a lump in her throat. She had been blessed to find a job with a boss as kind and understanding as Carol.

Lauren watched as each employee was handed a gift. Carol read Lauren's name and handed her a square box wrapped in bright Christmas bells. Since everyone held a different shaped gifted, Lauren knew they were individually chosen by their employer. Lauren could not imagine what was inside her box.

When everyone had been gifted, Carol gave the okay to open. Lauren pulled out a calf-length, light brown, puffer coat with a faux fur lined hood. It would be much warmer than the leather jacket she wore now. It had lost its sheen years ago after a decade of wear. The new coat was nicer and much warmer.

Lauren held out the worn bottom of her jacket and asked Carol, "How did you know?"

Carol's sly smile spoke volumes. "You shiver every day when you come in and you head straight for the hot coffee."

"This is so wonderful. Thank you."

After everyone had chorused their thanks for a hand-picked gift, Carol said, "Open the card attached to your present."

When they did, they discovered a crisp one-hundred-dollar bill tucked inside. Last year there had been a twenty-five-dollar gift card for a department store." This is too much," Lauren gasped.

"We've had a good year and decided to pass some of the blessing along to our employees," Carol said. "There may not be as much next year."

Lauren considered the profit and loss records she'd been keeping. It had been a good year/

She added her thanks to the chorus around her. The money would go towards buying Christmas dinner and paying for Jeffrey's. sitter expenses during Christmas break.

Tears filled her eyes. "Thank you, Carol. This helps a lot."

"She tucked the money into her purse. When she had to pay the sitter and the bills for Jeffrey's Christmas gifts, she would have the funds.

The party gradually wound down. Folks were tired from the holiday rush and were soon helping clean up and grab left over's that we're divided into Styrofoam containers to take home. Lauren accepted her portion gratefully.

"I put a little extra in yours since you liked it so much," Beth said, smiling at Lauren.

"Thanks, Beth. It won't go to waste. We'll eat them for supper tomorrow."

"Let me know when it's your birthday and I'll make you some more," Beth offered.

"That's generous, but only if you let me know when it's your birthday, too."

Beth grinned at her. The wrinkles around her eyes crinkled. 'You have a deal."

Lauren glanced at her watch. It was almost nine o'clock. After three hours with Abby and Vic, she was afraid Jeffrey would outstay his welcome.

She slipped into her new coat and enjoyed its blessed warmth on the way to her car. Such a coat was not something she would have gotten for herself and she was grateful Carol had provided it since the cold wind that cut across the parking lot would have chilled her to the bone in her leather jacket. As it was, she pulled the coat hood atop her head and felt snug.

She listened to Christmas carols as she drove to pick up Jeffrey. She hoped he hadn't been too much for the elderly couple. They were lovely people, and she didn't want to take advantage of them.

The front porch light lent a welcoming beacon when Lauren parked in the driveway. She walked to the porch and rang the bell. Vic answered.

"You're here to pick up our boy," he said. "We've had a jolly good time."

Jeffrey appeared beside him. "Do we have to go, Mom? I've had so much fun. We made sugar cookies and played checkers and chess and they loved a picture I drew."

"I'm so glad, honey. We do have to go now."

"Aww." Jeffrey looked as though he would balk.

Lauren tensed, hoping he didn't pitch a fit.

Vic put his arm around Jeffrey's shoulders. "Don't you worry son. We'll have another checker match the next time you stay with us. You go along nice now."

Jeffrey nodded and slipped into his coat.

Abby appeared with a bag of sugar cookies in her hand. "Here you two. Eat these up so Vic and I don't," she said.

Jeffrey reached for them without hesitation. "They're good, Mom."

"Thank you so much for all you've done tonight. May I pay you a little something for your time?"

They both gave their heads a vigorous shake. "Absolutely not," Abby said. "We love having Jeffrey. Are you two going to church with us tomorrow?"

"I wouldn't miss it," Lauren said, and smiled.

She led Jeffrey to the car, and they hopped in out of the wind. Jeffrey snuggled into the seat. "I had so much fun. They're the best friends ever. I'm glad I didn't have to stay with Ruby. She's no fun at all. All she does is eat and watch television."

Lauren started the car. "You'll still have to stay with Ruby sometimes."

Jeffrey sighed. "I know, but I wish I didn't."

He sniffed. "What smells so good? Kinda cheesy."

"Beth at work made the best enchiladas for dinner tonight. She let me bring some home."

"May I have some now?"

They parked in the drive. Jeffrey turned to the back seat, twisting so he could get a strong whiff.

"You said you were full," Lauren reminded him. "Let's save them for lunch tomorrow. We can share with Grandma Abby and Grandpa Vic."

"Okay. That will be fun. I hope I'm hungry, though. Grandma makes a big breakfast."

Lauren could just make out the profile of her growing boy in the automatic light inside the garage. She pulled toward it to park inside. He had been a baby such a short time ago. She suspected he'd be looking down on her in three or four years. His dad had been a hulk of a man, over six foot two and big.

In the relative warmth of the closed garage, they piled from the car. Lauren retrieved the enchiladas and slid them into the refrigerator in the kitchen. While Jeffrey got ready for bed, she checked the weather forecast for the next day. A snowstorm was predicted overnight but clearing by morning. If the grandparents' driveway was covered, they would have to shovel it before church. She supposed Jeffrey wouldn't mind. He didn't seem to mind doing anything for them. If only he was that cooperative for her, it would be an answer to the prayer she'd sent up last Sunday.

After Jeffrey went to bed, she sat in the living room and gazed at their lit Christmas tree. The cup of hot tea she held in her hands warmed her body as the peace of Christmas filled her heart. In her hectic daily life, she forgot all the things she had for which to be thankful. She had a job and a terrific boss, a warm home and food in the kitchen and she had Jeffrey. He was hard at times. Yet, she wouldn't trade him. His small acts of sweetness over the years were encouragements. Lately, she was seeing more of them.

Before she went to bed, she looked out the window to see the flakes falling in a dense curtain of white. "Not too much," she whispered. "I don't want to be stuck inside all morning."

She dumped the dregs of her tea and headed to bed, wondering if she'd wake to a wonderland with snow-packed roads.

CHAPTER SEVEN

Krista rose on Sunday morning to see a front yard covered with snow. She smiled as she thought about the beautiful evening, she'd had Friday night with Trent. After supper at an Italian restaurant, they had driven the city to see the Christmas lights. They'd each chosen their favorite and compared their choices on the way home. Krista had asked Trent about his family's Christmas traditions and she had shared her family's traditions.

"Traditions are important," she said. "They bring families together year after year even when they're far apart. Some of my friends and I touch base only once or twice a year and it's always at Christmas or birthdays."

"When is your birthday?" Trent had asked.

"It's in February. How about you?"

"I turned twenty-seven on December fifth."

"I just missed your birthday," she said. "I turned twenty-six last February eleventh."

He clicked his tongue. "Just a child."

She shook her head. "Yes, So much younger than you."

It had been a fun evening and the bowling they had done on Saturday afternoon had been fun, too. He'd had to be home by five o'clock on Saturday and hadn't told her the reason. Because of that, a worrisome thought had niggled its way into her mind. Did he have a date? The thought of it put a stab through her stomach. it would not be dishonorable if he had gone out with someone else. She and Trent had no understanding. Yet the idea of him seeing another woman made her feel ill.

She dressed in warm sweats and sat at the kitchen table to drink a mug of coffee. She collected Christmas mugs and this one had a jolly Santa dressed in red as the image. "I know what I want for Christmas," she told him. "I don't know if you can fit him in a box."

At ten o'clock, her phone rang. She expected it to be her mom. Instead, it was Trent.

"Hey," he said. "I hope I didn't wake you."

"No. I've been up for a while."

"Good. "I didn't want to wake you. I'm taking my mom to church at eleven and then helping her set up her Christmas tree. I want to invite you to do either or both with us. Feel free to say no if you don't want to. I'll understand."

Krista's heart jumped. "I'd love to meet your mom and help her with her tree and a Christmas church service would be wonderful. I go to the Christmas Eve service with my parents, but I'm free this morning."

"Great. May I swing by about ten-thirty?"

"Sure. I'll be ready."

Krista went into hyper drive after they hung up. She had twenty minutes to change clothes and do her hair and make-up. Though she had readily agreed to go, jitters formed in her stomach about meeting his mom. What if she was the judgmental type and didn't like Krista? That would lead to an awkward and uncomfortable afternoon. She shook away the thought. It was silly to worry before she even met the woman. If she and Trent kept dating, it was inevitable that she and his mother would meet. It might as well be now.

She curled her shoulder-length brown hair and fluffed her bangs into a curl above her eyebrows. She slipped into a long-sleeved blue dress with a lacy collar and then into her calf-length brown coat that was fuzzy enough to keep her warm.

When Trent showed up, she was already waiting at the door.

"I'm glad you could come," he said.

He took in her appearance and smiled. "I'm glad you wore a warm coat. It's twenty-degrees out here."

"If I could, I would skip from fall to spring," she said.

Trent raised a brow. "You're not a fan of winter, huh? Not even for skiing?"

"Never been. I've cared for a lot of patients with ski injuries, though."

"I've skied since I was six without crashing into a tree or breaking a bone."

She shook her head.

"I haven't convinced you, have I?" he asked.

"Nope. You've been lucky."

She wasn't surprised that he skied. His lean athletic build would be an asset in any sport. His positive nature suggested he would expect a good outcome from anything he tried. Her experience caring for sports injuries and all sorts of accidents suggested otherwise.

She snuggled into his warm car. The heated seat felt amazing. The heater in her car worked, but there was nothing else warm about it.

"You said you moved here from Texas when you were sixteen. That was a big adjustment going from there to chilly Colorado. What was your first thought?"

"You won't take offense?"

He smiled. "Nope."

"I hated it. It was my junior year, and I didn't know anyone. I was mad at my parents until I made new friends. I love it here now."

"What brought you here?"

"My folks are both in real estate. My mom sells houses, and my dad works in wildlife conservation. He got an offer from a company here and decided to take it."

When Trent only nodded, she said, "You work in construction. Would you two be in competition?"

"Not necessarily. It depends on where they are developing. There do have to be areas where the animals are protected."

She was relieved by his reasonable answer. "Like Estes State Park. We drove over one weekend and my folks decided to take a hike. I stayed in the car and some moose began grazing in front of me. I watched them for a half-hour before they moved on. They had cute, braided fur that hung down from their chins. All my parents saw were squirrels and chipmunks."

"Do you like camping?" Trent asked.

Krista thought about past camping trips. "We only went a few times with a club I was in. I liked it okay as long as there was running water. I don't think I'd like dry camping."

"You see a lot of wildlife when you're not close to other people. One time a black bear wandered into camp. He sniffed around a while and then left. We had our food tied out of reach in a tree."

Krista shivered as she imagined the scene. "How old were you?"

"About ten. My dad was an outdoorsman. He taught my brother and me how to survive off the land."

"That's a good skill to have." Krista thought she could survive a day or maybe two if left alone in the wilderness."

"Black bears can climb trees. Why didn't he climb up and eat your food?" Krista asked.

"The branches were too small to hold his weight."

"I see. I would have been terrified, weren't you?"

His expression became wistful. "I wasn't scared. I trusted my dad to take care of us. There wasn't anything I thought he couldn't do."

"I'm close to my parents, too. Still, I wouldn't have thought my father could take on a bear. He wasn't as skilled in the outdoors as your dad."

Trent signaled a right turn and maneuvered deftly into the left lane. Heavy traffic unsettled Krista. She was glad she wasn't driving. The crowded road didn't seem to bother Trent.

"Do your parents still camp?" she asked.

"My dad died three years ago from a sudden heart attack. My mom has no interest in it without him."

I'm so sorry. That must have been awful."

Trent nodded. "It was pretty bad. Holidays are still hard for us."

Krista's heart ached for him. "Would it help to do something different this year? Spend Christmas with my folks and me?"

He stopped at a light and gazed into her eyes. "That's awfully kind. I'll ask my mom. After she meets you, I'll be surprised if she doesn't agree."

His words touched her heart. She was falling hard for this dark-haired, blue-eyed man. In the brief time they'd been dating she'd memorized the curve of his cheeks, his strong chin, and the dimple on the left side of his chin.

They drove another two blocks before turning onto a street with small brick homes and tall pines. He pulled into the driveway of a house on the right side of the street. It had a picture window in the front and two smaller windows on the other side of a front door painted wine red.

How long has your mom lived here?" Krista asked.

"Thirty-four years. They bought it seven years before I was born."

"That's a long time to be in one place."

"They loved the house and the neighborhood and never had a reason to move."

This painted a romantic picture in Krista's mind of a cozy home and neighborhood children playing and growing up together. At Christmas, she imagined a tree in the same corner of the living room each year with a growing collection of childhood decorations each year.

Before they reached the door, a dark-haired woman popped out. She wore a long white coat and golden bell earrings. Her sky-blue eyes told Krista that Trent favored his mom.

She smiled at Krista as she rushed forward to greet her. "You must be Krista. I'm so pleased to meet you. You are as pretty as Trent said."

"Thank you, Mrs. Dryden."

"Call me Amanda. Mrs. Dryden sounds too old."

"Then thank you, Amanda. It's nice to meet you, too."

They strolled through the still brisk sunlit morning. A few alabaster clouds played chase across the vivid blue sky. Krista didn't feel as cold on clear brisk mornings as she did when the sky was gray, and it muted the colors of the trees and buildings. Even if the temperature was colder on clear days, it seemed warmer than the darker days.

At Trent's car, Krista opened the back door and prepared to take the back seat. Amanda gently grasped her arm. "Oh no, dear. You sit in front with Trent. Otherwise, I'll feel like an old lady. That will put me into a funk and none of us want that."

Her eyes were warm and teasing. Krista smiled back. "I certainly do not want to offend you. I'll take the front."

Krista noticed Trent grinning as he listened to the exchange. The nervousness she'd felt about meeting Amanda had all but evaporated. She seemed a lovely lady and had put Krista at ease. As Trent started the car, Krista turned to Amanda. "Trent tells me you've lived here over thirty years. That's rare now. You must like this neighborhood."

Amanda wore a wistful smile. "We've always loved it When we first moved in, it was a new area. There were lots of young families with little kids. Trent and his brother had many friends to play with. They played touch football in the front yard and baseball in a vacant lot down the street. There were plenty of kids to make teams. Samuel and I had couples over and we all went to baseball games with our kids. Now, neighborhoods can be full of lonely people, but ours wasn't then."

"That's so nice," Krista mused. "I was lonely when my folks and I moved here. It took a while to make friends."

"What? A lovely girl like you? That's hard to imagine."

Krista loved her flattery. "Thank you. It was hard for a while, though."

"You like it here now, right?" Trent asked.

The slight note of concern in his voice made Krista wonder if he thought she had a desire to move away. Now that she'd been here for the last few years, she'd grown attached to the town. Her parents were here and so were her friends.

In answer to Trent, she said, "It was hard to be uprooted in high school. However, I love it here now."

Her answer made him smile. He had a nice smile. The curve of his smile brought out the dimple on his chin. With his easy disposition and handsome features, she wondered why he wasn't married. Surely, more than one woman had set her sights on him. Perhaps, like herself, he hadn't met the person with whom he wanted to share the rest of his life.

They turned the corner on South Central Street, to enter one of the oldest parts of the city. Many of the brick buildings were built close together and dated back to the early nineteen hundreds. A pharmacy that housed an original soda fountain, a bank, jewelry store, and a furniture store were a few of the first stores in the city. Krista didn't get to this part of town often and admired the handsome gray brick structures when she had reason to come here.

The church stood at the end of the block. The brownstone building was two stories with a lovely steeple and white concrete steps that led to oaken double doors. Though she'd never been inside, Krista had always thought it was the prettiest church in town.

"Is this where you've always gone to church?" she asked.

"Trent's dad and I were married in this church and the boys were raised going here," Amanda replied. "We've had three pastors during the time we've come here, and we loved each of them. We have good friends here, people who stand by us in good times and bad times. That's something I never take for granted," Amanda said.

"It also has secret passages that kids love to explore," Trent said as he maneuvered the car into a parking space in the lot behind the church.

"That sounds intriguing," Krista said.

"In the back of the choir room, we could open a door that led up a flight of stairs to a storage room overlooking the parking lot. The door on the other side of the room opens to a stairwell that leads to an exit on the ground floor of the church," Trent said.

"Where were you supposed to be when you were doing all this exploring?" Amanda asked.

"Usually in Sunday School or choir," Trent said.

"Did that ever get you in trouble?" Krista asked.

He nodded. "Oh, yes."

When they left the warm car, their breath came out in white puffs. They strode briskly toward the church whose white steeple rose above the pitched roof to point a white spire at the sky. When they reached the concrete steps, they were greeted by two white-haired gentlemen in wool overcoats who shook their hands and opened one of the polished oak doors to admit them into the foyer. Cozy warmth enfolded Krista like a warm comforter as the chill left her bones. She accompanied Trent and his mother into a sanctuary adorned by gold and silver garlands that draped the pews. Each pew had artificial poinsettias fastened at each end while the altar held lush red poinsettias

Krista took a mental picture of the setting to treasure among her Christmas memories. Though she should not plan on it, she desired that Trent and Amanda would become more than brief recollections.

As they trod down the aisle, she spotted the elderly couple who lived next door. A woman, and a boy who looked like the ones who lived on the other side of her, sat with them. Krista smiled and nodded, and they smiled back.

"Do you know some of the congregation?" Amanda asked.

Krista scanned the rows of unfamiliar faces. "Only the folks I just saw. They are neighbors."

"I love seeing familiar faces and new ones, too," Amanda said.

Trent stopped at a pew on their right with empty seats beside them. Amanda went in first, then Krista. Trent sat on the end. On this cold day, Krista welcomed the heat from his body and wished it would be appropriate to snuggle closer.

The choir began with the traditional carol, "O Come All Ye Faithful. The sopranos gave her goose bumps at the crescendo of the last chorus. "Oh, come let us adore Him, Christ the Lord."

The congregation was invited to stand and sing more carols. It brought Krista back to childhood memories of practicing them on the piano for a Christmas recital when she was a child. Her parents had given her the piano when she moved to her own house.

After the singing, a middle-aged man in a beige sports coat stepped forward to mount the three steps to the altar and take the podium. He read a verse from the Christmas story and then led the congregation in prayer.

Krista had been on edge about attending the church. Now, she began to relax.

The sermon covered the true meaning of Christmas and how it often got lost in the busy stress or business goals of the season. Krista could sympathize with the stress. The hospital usually saw an increase in vehicle accident victims as well as pneumonia and flu. The strain on the families affected Krista when she'd worked Christmas Eve last year. She was grateful she didn't work it this year.

After the sermon, the same gentleman who had done the Scripture reading read the announcements in the bulletin. Afterwards, church ended with "O Little Town of Bethlehem".

Krista, Trent, and Amanda filed out with the congregation. In the foyer, several groups of people gathered to talk. Since Krista didn't know anyone, she was glad Amanda and Trent didn't stop to chat.

The sun had warmed the air by the time they walked to the car. "What did you think of the service?" Trent asked.

"I loved it. When I was a kid, we went to the Christmas Eve service. After we moved here, we quit going. I forgot how much I enjoyed Christmas church services until now."

"I'm very glad you came with us this morning," Amanda said.

Trent took Krista's hand and gave it a gentle squeeze. "I'm glad, too."

On the way back to Amanda's house, Trent pulled into a diner. Since the front of the lot was filled, he pulled to the side and found a space to park. Krista hadn't realized they would be going out to lunch. Her stomach awoke with a gentle gurgle at the prospect of food.

"They have plate lunches, burgers, and sandwiches. Do you think you'd like to eat here? We come here a lot after church, and they have good food."

"I think I would love it," Krista answered.

They piled from the car and headed around the sidewalk to the front door of the shiny, metal, building with a steep roof like a Swiss chalet. Windows on every side allowed them a peek at the customers already seated at tables.

"I hope there's room for us," Krista said.

"It's bigger than it looks on the outside," Amanda assured her. "It goes back farther than you would think."

"We've never been turned away," Trent said, "at least not yet."

Trent held the door for Krista and his mom when they entered. Krista's mouth reacted to the scent of fried meat and potatoes and the sweet smell of homemade ice cream advertised by a sign behind the glassed-in case.

They were third in line before a young woman greeted them in front of the check-out.

"Would you like a table or booth?" she asked.

Amanda and Trent looked at Krista. She hated decisions like this. If one of them had a preference, she would rather they decide.

"I don't mind either," she said.

Trent eased her discomfort by saying, "We'll take a table, please."

The hostess' sapphire nose ring wiggled when she smiled. "Very good. Come this way."

Krista admired the shine of the girl's dark hair. It fell in soft waves down her back that undulated when she walked. If Krista had hair like that, she would wear her hair long and loose instead of shoulder length and layered. They seated themselves at the table with Krista, once again, between Trent and Amanda. The hostess handed them menus and promised a waiter soon.

Krista's hunger peaked when she looked at the full-color pictures of some of the classics. A bacon cheeseburger, turkey and Swiss, and grilled ham on croissants were pictured with plump fries and a juicy dill pickle.

She perused the other choices and decided on a grilled chicken sandwich with guacamole. Her next choice would be fruit bowl or fries. Should she be good and stick to the diet that she'd followed for the last two years or allow herself the fried treat she had avoided?

She would see what Trent and Amanda ordered and follow their lead.

When they compared their choices, it seemed Trent was drawn to the bacon cheeseburger while Amanda favored the Swiss and grilled ham.

The waitress approached their table wearing a smile that seemed permanently fixed on her face. Her name tag labeled her as Trish. When she asked if they wanted fruit or fries, Trent answered, "Fries."

"Fruit," said Amanda.

Krista made a quick decision. I'll go with the fruit."

Tall and thin, Trish moved gracefully away. Krista thought this must be one of the hardest jobs to do. She doubted she'd last a day at it. She'd worked at a stable as a teen and far preferred it.

Amanda turned to Krista. "Tell me about yourself. Trent tells me you're a nurse. That's about all I know. In what part of the hospital do you work?"

"I work in the operating room. It can be intense."

Amanda nodded." I bet it is. How do you like working with doctors?"

Krista wanted to be honest. "You can't be thin-skinned. Some of them are gruff. Most of them are okay to work with."

Amanda shook her head. "I could never do that job. I'm too squeamish."

Trent jumped into the conversation. "What made you want to go into nursing?"

After thinking a moment, Krista said, "I've always been fascinated by how things work. I

don't have the aptitude to be a mechanic or engineer, and the miracle of the human body

fascinates me. So, I chose nursing."

"We need more good nurses like you," Amanda said.

"Thank you." Krista glanced at Trent and he captured her gaze and smiled.

Their food arrived shortly after the conversation. After they admired the way it looked, Trent said a blessing.

Then, he said, "I'm hungry enough to eat three of these."

His mother shook her head. "No, you aren't, but I bet you'll finish what you have."

She turned to Krista and added. "He was a picky eater as a kid. Fortunately, he grew out of it."

"I'm afraid I was a bit of a spoiled eater since I'm an only child. My mom usually made things I liked. I wasn't terribly picky, though," Krista said.

"Good. I'd like to have you and Trent stay for dinner tonight if you have time. I worried a bit about offending your taste buds. I cook pretty simple homey foods."

"That's my favorite kind," Krista answered.

She bit into her sandwich and enjoyed the rich taste of the grilled chicken topped with spicy guacamole. Her lunches at home were so plain that this tasted gourmet. On her days off, she often had a bowl of cereal. At work, she grabbed a grilled cheese in the cafeteria. This was miles above either of those choices.

Trent said, "Krista and I met when she brought Angel home. Apparently, Angel decided she would rather live with Krista and paid her a visit."

Amanda chuckled. "If you've spent much time with Angel, you know she is a beggar for attention. If she isn't bringing you a ball, she's begging to be petted."

"She was very sweet and she's a beautiful dog. I'm sure her fur takes a lot of work. She always looks brushed out,"

"That's because I brush her every night after work. She protested when she was a puppy. She's used to it now," Trent said.

"I'd like to brush her sometime," Krista said. "I've always liked to brush hair."

Trent chuckled. "You may brush her all you like. It's a chore for me even though I like the way she looks when I'm done."

"Let me know when you want her done again. Tomorrow, maybe?"

"You got a date."

Her cheeks warmed when she realized she had invited herself over."

"Only if you don't have other plans," she added.

"I don't. We can have supper and watch a Christmas movie while you brush Angel if that sounds fun."

"Sure. What can I bring?"

"Not a thing," Amanda broke in. "I have leftover chicken cordon bleu from dinner last Wednesday. I froze it but won't use it all. If you like, I can send rolls and noodles, too."

"I do like," Trent said.

"It sounds wonderful. At least let me bring a salad," Krista said.

Trent smiled. "If you bring a salad, I won't have to do a thing."

Amanda slapped his hand with a napkin. "Lazy boy," she said with a grin.

Krista polished off the rest of her sandwich and her second glass of sweet peach tea. She would barely have room to eat her bowl of fruit.

When Trent asked if anyone wanted dessert, Krista shook her head. "I'm not sure I can finish this fruit".

She speared the last strawberry and set down her fork, leaving two pieces of watermelon and a chunk of cantaloupe.

"I can finish it for you," Trent said.

Amanda huffed. "That's not polite."

This made Krista chuckle. "It's all right. I don't mind."

The tall waitress with the permanent smile gave them their check." Thank you for coming in. Be sure and come back soon."

"We will," Amanda said.

Their little group collected at the cash register and Trent paid the tab.

The day had warmed to be comfortable in coats as they walked to the car. Krista thought she'd need a lot more exercise after that meal. She would do it tomorrow with a long walk around the neighborhood.

They chatted about their Christmas traditions on the way home. Amanda said, "We always put our Christmas lights on the house the weekend after Thanksgiving. One year, the boys were going to help their father hang the lights as usual."

Trent groaned. "I know where this is going."

Krista grinned at him. "I want to hear this"

Amanda beamed. "It's a doozy."

"I can't wait," Krista said.

Amanda cleared her throat. "It happened like this. The boys decided to play a trick. They worked half a day with their dad getting the lights up on the house and trees in the front yard. Then, they took turns turning off the breaker when their dad plugged in the lights. They would be on for a while and mysteriously go off. "

"There was steam coming from his ears," Trent said. "Then, after a few minutes, he saw the humor and started laughing."

"If I remember right," Amanda said, "he made you two boys take them down and pack them away that year."

Trent nodded. "He said if we were old enough to manage the breaker, we were old enough to put away the lights. It was a big job, and we were wondering if it was worth the fun of the trick."

"Your poor dad." Krista shook her head.

"Bet you never did anything like that," Trent said.

"Not even remotely," she agreed.

When they got back to the house, it was mid-afternoon. Krista wondered how long it would take to put up the tree and get the decorations in place. It didn't truly matter because she had nothing to do that evening and plenty of time.

They parked in the driveway. The sun was still high in the sky and made a glowing effect on the front windows of the house. A mild breeze rustled the branches of the tall pines and pine dropped pinecones crunched underfoot as they crossed the yard.

Amanda put her key in the lock and opened the front door. Once they stepped inside the warmth of the house enveloped them like a cozy duvet.

The rectangular living room lay bare of any Christmas decorations. The country style sofa with wing back arms and matching armchair sat together opposite the plate-glass window that opened to a view of the street and front yard. The walnut coffee table in front of the couch held hard-back books of National Parks and magazines about home décor. A wall-mounted television sat next to one window while a stereo system lay on the other side of the window. Krista wondered what sort of music Amanda liked. Krista's mom liked classical music. Perhaps Amanda's tastes were different.

Amanda pointed to the right corner of the living room. "We'll put the tree there, as usual."

"I know my cue," Trent said. "Up to the attic to bring down the boxes."

Amanda patted her son on the shoulder. "Like a good boy. Thank you."

Trent took the hallway that led from the living room to the back of the house. While he was gone Amanda turned on Christmas music for them to listen to while they decorated the tree. "I love this time of year," she said.

Krista looked out the window at the crisp, blue, winter sky. "I do, too."

Trent returned with a long cardboard box in his arms. He set it near the corner of the living room. "Here's the tree. We'll start with this. Then, I'll go back up for the ornaments."

He turned to Krista. "I'll warn you, my mom has a lot of Christmas decorations."

He slit open the tape on the box and they pulled out the tree. Since it was pre-lit, they wouldn't have to take the time to untangle and string on the lights as she'd done for her parents. It was the hardest part of setting up their tree.

Trent pulled it from the box and smoothed out the white branches. Krista tried to imagine what it would look like all decorated. It would surely be beautiful.

Trent grinned at the women and sighed a long-suffering sigh. "Back to the attic."

Amanda rolled her eyes and told Krista. "It's not that bad. There's a nice pull-down ladder in the hallway and the attic is floored in."

"I take back any sympathy I was tempted to feel," Krista said.

Trent returned a few minutes later with a bulky box. "This grows every year."

"It does not," Amanda said. "I haven't bought new Christmas ornaments in years. You're getting older, my dear."

Trent shook his head. "Can't be that."

When he opened the box, Krista peered inside at the lovely shiny balls and golden garland. "I can't wait to see these on the tree."

"I finally convinced her to leave off the homemade ornaments my brother and I made in school twenty years ago. They were getting ragged."

"I still have them saved in a box," Amanda said.

"My mom still puts them on their tree," Krista said.

"I bet they are precious," Amanda said.

They began the process of winding the garland and placing the red and blue balls on the branches. White lace bows and ceramic angels went on next. They finished by adding tinsel to sparkle on every branch. When they stood back and viewed it, the effect was gorgeous.

"I think we did a very nice job," Amanda said,

"It looks amazing," Krista said.

"I'll clear away these boxes and get the manger. I know you'll want it next," Trent said.

Amanda told Krista, "It goes on the coffee table."

Trent exaggerated a stagger under the empty boxes. "I'll be right back."

He returned with the manger. They opened it and gingerly removed the pieces.

"They look so delicate," Krista said.

"They are china and a gift from my late husband. I had always wanted a set like this."

"I'm afraid to touch them," Krista said.

"She doesn't let me touch them," Trent said.

Krista raised a brow. "I wonder why."

Amanda carefully arranged Mary and Joseph nearest Jesus. The angels stood behind them and the shepherds and three sheep stood looking on at the scene.

"I think we have it," Amanda said. "How about if I make some hot chocolate and we sit a bit in the living room to enjoy our work? Do you have time, Krista?"

Krista had nothing pressing to do the rest of the afternoon. "That would be great."

Amanda beamed. "You two sit and I'll be right back."

"She really likes you. The next time you're here, she'll probably shove us under the mistletoe."

Krista knew her chuckle sounded nervous.

"Would that be so bad?" he asked.

She answered honestly. "No. It wouldn't."

They watched a Christmas movie and Amanda made a simple supper of tacos and corn, with leftover chocolate cake for dessert."

After supper, they played a game of dominoes before Trent took her home. He kissed her at her doorway, and it was anything except bad. It was wonderful, gentle, and lingering, the scent of his aftershave making her heady. If she'd had any doubt about her feelings for him they evaporated at that moment.

After he left, she gave her mom a call and explained that she'd invited Trent and his mother for Christmas Day."

"I'm sure that would be lovely," her mom said. "What are their names?"

"Trent and Amanda Dryden."

"Oh dear," said her mom. "I'm not sure that will work."

CHAPTER EIGHT

Lauren had enjoyed church with Jeffrey, Vic, and Abby on Sunday morning. It was good for Jeffrey to be with the other kids and Lauren had been uplifted by the message. She was getting to know some of the congregation and had even seen the young woman who lived next door with the man who lived on the other side of her and an older woman. Were they dating, perhaps? If so, she wished them well.

After church, she'd taken Jeffrey bowling. She wasn't good at it and couldn't teach him much, yet he enjoyed it and it worked off his energy. They'd stopped for supper at a burger place and then drove around a few neighborhoods to look at Christmas lights. Every year Jeffrey asked to put them on their house. Every year she gave the same answer. Lights would be too expensive and too much trouble. Maybe when he was older and could do most of the work, they would try it, if the lights weren't too expensive. In the meantime, they would enjoy the work of others.

They had agreed on the favorite display of white lights all around the front yard fence and around the roof of the house. The yard had lit reindeer that moved their necks in a grazing motion. The pine tree in their yard had red and white lights with a glowing yellow star at the top.

On the way home, Jeffrey asked when he could go Christmas shopping. Lauren wished that he would forget. It was more trouble than it was worth to take him to get a small gift for her. He usually had not saved much of his allowance and asked for a loan that he later balked about. It would be better if he would forego her gift. Yet he usually insisted.

She sighed. "I don't know, honey. Why don't you make me something this year? You could write a poem or make a soup and sandwich dinner. I would like something like that."

"I could do that, too, I have something that I really want to get you, though."

"Do you have the money for it? I'm not doing another loan."

"I do. Honest."

Lauren guessed he would probably be surprised at what her gift cost and end up asking for money. "I'd prefer something you make."

"Nope. This idea is good."

"All right. We'll go tomorrow evening."

She was going to be tired from work and sorry she'd made the promise. Yet Jeffrey could be very persistent, and she'd have no peace if she denied him.

When they got home, he got ready for bed without an argument...until she gave him the bad news. "You're on holiday tomorrow and I'm not. You'll have to spend the day with Ruby."

His frown turned his face into a thundercloud.

"I hate being with her. She's so boring. She never plays chess or bakes treats or lets me do anything except read or watch television."

"I know, honey. Try to have a good attitude for my sake. I wish I could do better for you, but I don't have anyone else to ask. You can't spend all day with our neighbors while I'm at work. They are older people, and they get tired."

He sighed. "I'd rather be with them, but I don't want them to get tired. They might die and it would be my fault."

Lauren hugged him. "Oh, honey. It's not your fault when someone dies. They are either old or sick or have an accident. You can't keep those things from happening."

"I don't want them to die. I just got them."

"I know, honey. Try not to worry. They seem healthy to me."

THE NEXT DAY WAS A long one at work. Yearend statements were due, and she wanted to get as much done as possible before Christmas to save herself stress. However, so many receipts came in that she hardly had time to start on the reports. She still had more than a week before Christmas Eve. Hopefully, she'd catch a break before then.

She ate lunch at her desk. She'd hoped to work, yet ended up talking with her mom, who was in Morocco visiting bazaars with her husband. Nothing excited Mom more than a good bargain or unique gifts.

She said, "I found you and Jeffrey some of the cutest belts and scarves and I won't tell you what else. I want to surprise you for Christmas, even if they'll arrive a little late. I just mailed them today."

Though her mom rarely saw Lauren on her birthday or holidays, she often sent earrings from the country she was visiting. The ones from Spain were made from red and black grillwork in the shape of a rose. Lauren thought they would look nice with her black classic dress. Perhaps, one day someone would ask her to a place to wear them.

"Thanks, Mom. I'm sure we'll love the gifts. She'd never admit that she'd sold most of them at garage sales over the years. The extra cash came in handy and it wasn't as if her mom would ever notice since she hardly ever came to visit.

"What are you and Jeffrey doing for Christmas?"

Lauren took a calming breath. She was determined not to let the bitterness she felt creep into her voice. It had never done any good to complain. Her mom only got defensive and made angry excuses as to why she and Lauren's stepdad had to travel while they still had the health to do it.

Lauren understood...sort of.

In answer to her mother's questions, she said, "Jeffrey and I are spending the morning with some neighbors on Christmas. They are a lovely older couple, and Jeffrey adores them. "

"That's wonderful, honey. I hope Jeffrey is not too much for them. Last time we saw him he was a rather difficult child. How's his temper doing now?"

"Better. I think they've been good for him. He likes them so much that he doesn't want to disappoint them."

"That's wonderful. I hope it lasts." She didn't sound convinced.

So much for moral support. Lauren's goal for the last eight years had been to see Jeffrey blossom into a young man of self-control. Now that it seemed to be happening, she didn't need discouragement.

They chatted about Morocco for a few more minutes before hanging up. Lauren fought the dark cloud hanging over her after speaking with her mom. The brown paneled walls of her small office closed around her in a suffocating claustrophobic vice until her gaze shifted to the two. landscape photos she'd cut from an art magazine she'd gotten as a sample in the mail. She'd tacked them to the wall to relieve the brown tedium surrounding her.

One photo showed a river running through a deep canyon between two mountains. The sky above was azure blue with a few puffy clouds. In the crags of the foreground, a few mountain goats grazed the scattered grass. The other painting featured a blue lake that reflected the shadow of a mountain. They were peaceful, quiet scenes because that's how she liked to experience the outdoors. No extreme river rafting or rock climbing for her. She preferred a quiet walk along a woodland path or a drive along country roads to view fall colors.

Disquiet caused by her mother's call faded and she focused her attention back to the receipts. If she was going to meet her goal of getting these done and starting on the reports, she would have to forget about her mother's call and concentrate on her work.

She'd made decent progress by five o'clock. She grabbed her warm new coat that Carol had bought her and locked her door. She wished Carol and the cashiers a good evening and headed out to pick up Jeffrey. Hopefully, she'd get more done tomorrow than she had today.

Ruby wore a scowl when she opened the door. "He was a grouch all day and complained about everything. He didn't like his lunch. He didn't want to watch what he was allowed. He tried to talk me into a show that I didn't know was okay. Then he argued. When I sent him to the backyard to play, he grouched about it being too cold. I don't know how long I can do this."

Lauren felt a moment of panic. "It's only a few more days and then you'll only have him afterschool. Please don't quit on me. I don't have anyone else to watch him."

Ruby heaved a deep sigh. "It's going to cost you more if he doesn't start behaving better."

Lauren's stomach dropped. With money so tight it would be hard to afford more money for a sitter. She would have to talk to Jeffrey after supper. Now would not be good. When he was tired and hungry, he would only argue.

He remained silent most of the way home. Lauren didn't try to engage him in conversation. She'd learned that when he was tired or annoyed, he was more likely to fly into a screaming rage.

The sun set in a flaming red ball as they drove toward home. The trees along the boulevard of Main Street had shed their fall clothes of orange, red, and yellow. They stood bare and forlorn. They looked chilly without their covering as the wind blew them into twisted dancers whose spine was bent one way and then another.

They turned onto their block. Jeffrey was still. Lauren distracted herself from his dark mood by enjoying the Christmas lit houses with lights strung in their pines. Others had Santa, Nativities, or reindeer.

She pushed the button to close the automatic garage door and cringed as it ground its way down. It had been new when they first moved in. Now it sounded as though it was going to need work.

"Let's have supper," she said.

The door from the garage led directly into the kitchen. Not for the first time, she was glad they didn't have a detached garage.

Jeffrey plopped himself in a chair at the table that sat just past the garage door into the kitchen. Lauren let him defuse while she pulled out salad fixings and cold chicken she'd baked Sunday night. She opened boxed scalloped potatoes and set them to cook while she heated the chicken.

Jeffrey put his head on the table. He still hadn't said a word, Finally, he broke the silence. "I really hate being there. Please don't make me go back."

Lauren dreaded the discussion. "I wouldn't, honey, if I had anywhere else for you to stay."

Jeffrey raised his head. "Some of the kids go to a Boys and Girls Club. I heard about it at school. They were talking about playing games there while school was out. That would be better than Ruby's house. I bet it wouldn't cost any more than she charges.

Lauren's stomach clenched. She hated reminding him that his outbursts had kept him from mingling with the kids in daycare. She dreaded an argument in which he promised it wouldn't happen again only for him to backslide and get banned from yet another facility. Three daycares already wouldn't take him.

"I know it's hard for you not to lose your temper, but if you lost it there, they wouldn't let you come back."

"I won't. I promise."

Lauren had heard these words many times before and he'd never been able to do it. Every time she'd had to pick him up in disgrace and scramble to find another sitter. Right before Christmas was not the time she wanted to go through this drama again.

"Maybe we'll try it in the afternoons after Christmas. It's just a few more days."

Jeffrey scowled harder. "I promise I'll be okay. You don't believe me."

"I'd like to believe you, but we've tried before. It's hard for you."

"I know. I'm sorry. I've been a lot of trouble and that's why you don't think I can change. I can though"

" I do believe you can change. I just don't know if you're ready."

"You won't know unless you let me try. You can always send me back to Ruby." He made a face at her name.

"All right. I'll think about it. I'll call them tomorrow and see if they have an opening and how much it costs."

He perked up right away. "Thanks. That's great. You'll see. I won't cause any trouble."

The atmosphere in the kitchen brightened at his uplifted mood. Perhaps it was worth it. Even if the Boys and Girls Club didn't work out, they would have a pleasant evening tonight without more arguing.

"Can we watch a movie tonight," Jeffrey asked as he speared a bite of salad. It wasn't his favorite food. Tonight, he didn't complain about eating it.

"Sure. You have to go to bed at nine o'clock without asking to stay up later."

"I will. I promise."

"Okay. You may pick the movie as soon as we finish supper, and you help clean up the dishes."

He nodded. "Yes, Ma'am."

Lauren stared at him in surprise. He'd never called here ma'am before.

"That was polite," she said.

"Grandma Abby told me when she was a kid everybody said, ma'am and sir. I say it to her because she thinks it's polite."

"I think it's very nice," Lauren said. For the hundredth time, she blessed the grandparents for their influence on Jeffrey.

Right after the dishes were cleaned and the food put away, Lauren's phone rang. Her sister Lilly was calling. "How are you doing, Sis?" she asked.

"I'm doing okay. How about you?

Laruen motioned for Jeffrey to go and pick a movie. She mouthed, "I'll be there in a minute."

Jeffrey ambled to the living room and Lauren sank into a kitchen chair. Unlike her mom, Lilly was fun to talk to when she called. Lauren's regret was that her sister lived half-way across the country and they rarely saw one another.

"I'm doing great," Lilly answered her question. "I heard from Mom today. She told me they are in Morocco It sounds like she's having fun."

"She called me, too," Lauren said.

Lilly said, "She mentioned that. She told me she had a nice chat with you. Sometimes her idea of a nice chat is different than ours. Did you think it was nice?"

Lauren sighed. "Sometimes Mom has a way of making me feel bad when she's trying to be helpful, especially with Jeffrey."

"I know what you mean," Lilly said. "She told me that in the Christmas picture, Tommy looked like he was putting on too much weight. He's five foot ten and a hundred and fifty pounds. Does that sound like too much weight to you? "

"No. He still works out at the gym, doesn't he?"

"Yep, he's been a regular for ten years. Maybe she should worry about her own husband and not mine, "Lilly said.

"I really do love her, but it hurts my feelings that she and Stuart fly all over the world and she hasn't come to see me in over a year."

Lilly sighed. "I know. We saw them last April because their flight took off from Atlanta. They spent one night with us."

"I guess it's not worth getting upset. We can't change anything. I miss Dad, though," Lauren said.

"Me, too. How's work been going?"

They chatted about jobs and kids until Jeffrey began to call for Lauren.

"You said you were coming, and you've been on the phone forever," he complained.

"I know. I'm coming. Just a minute," Lauren called to him.

After talking about Christmas plans for a few more minutes, the sisters hung up. It had done Lauren a world of good to talk to Lilly. They were only a year and a half apart and had grown up like twins. Even when they'd fought, they worked it out quickly. Lilly was still Lauren's best friend.

She found Jeffrey sitting on the couch. He scowled at her as she came into the room. "You took forever."

"I don't get to talk to Aunt Lilly often and I miss her. We can still watch a short movie."

"Now it has to be short," he grumbled. "It's not fair."

Though it had annoyed Jeffrey, Lauren felt better after talking to Lilly.

She ignored his pout. Once he got into the movie, he'd be fine. Sure enough, fifteen minutes into, "How the Grinch Stole Christmas", Jeffrey was laughing and leaning against Lauren. Thanks to Dr. Seuss, her son had forgiven her for keeping him waiting.

It ended as it did every year with the Grinch having a change of heart. Though Lauren preferred A Christmas Carol as a story of a changed heart, Jeffrey loved The Grinch.

When it ended, Lauren reminded him it was time for bed. Perhaps she'd have time some evening left for her after he went to bed. She wanted to curl up on the couch, read her novel, and enjoy the Christmas tree.

"Time for bed," she told Jeffrey. Get into your pajamas and brush your teeth."

"It's only five minutes after nine o'clock. May I stay up fifteen minutes more!"

Lauren tensed. Here we go, she thought. He would pitch a fit when she stuck to her answer and ruin the rest of her evening until she thought of a strong enough punishment to convince him to do what she said. Then, she would suffer again when she followed through and he came unglued again.

Her tight neck and sour stomach would plague her for the rest of the evening. She envied couples who had each other for support with a challenging child. Though she tried to avoid self-pity, it had been hard to handle Jeffrey by herself.

She tried to keep her voice even. "We had a deal. You promised me you'd go to bed without a fuss. If you don't keep your word, I won't trust you the next time. I'll have to make your bedtime eight-thirty and we won't watch movies. Is that what you want?"

Jeffrey's face turned red. He opened his mouth to speak and then shut it. "Okay. I'm going to bed. I promised the grandparents I'd do what you say. Can I play on my i-Pad for a while?" he asked.

"Ten minutes and then turn it off," she said.

"Okay. Good-night, Mom."

"Good-night, honey. Sleep tight."

"I will."

Without another word, he turned and headed toward his room. He left Lauren on the couch, staring after him. Her muscles began to relax, and her stomach settled down. What had just happened? She'd told Lilly the grandparents down the block were good for him. Apparently, they were more like miracle workers. She'd have to tell them what a good influence they'd been.

She picked up her novel from the side table and pulled the fuzzy snowflake patterned fleece coverlet from the end of the couch. She pulled her legs under it and stared at the tree for a minute before picking up her book. The angel atop the tree seemed to smile down at her. Warmth crept through her and the sense of an all-powerful God who controlled all that she could not. It was okay to be small and not in control. God had put her here for a time and for a reason, and for the first time, she felt peace with her circumstances.

When she got so drifty, she couldn't keep her eyes open, she set down her book and went to her bedroom to change into the warm flannel gown with blue flowers. She brushed her teeth and snuggled under her thick comforter. Even though the sheets were chilly, she warmed quickly and fell asleep.

It seemed minutes until the alarm woke her at seven o-clock. She rose and made a cup of coffee before waking Jeffrey. "What do you want for breakfast?" she asked.

"Do I have time for pancakes?"

"Not today, but we can do that on Saturday."

He nodded and sat up."

"Get dressed and come get your breakfast," she said.

A few minutes later, he appeared in the kitchen and accepted a bowl of cold cereal. Lauren stuck a piece of bread in the toaster. When it stuck, as usual, she jiggled the lever to get it to pop up. It came out slightly darker than she preferred, but it would have to do. She smeared a pat of butter and a tablespoon of strawberry jam atop it and ate it while she checked messages on her cell phone. She had over twenty last minute Christmas sales alerts, two Merry Christmas messages from friends, and an offer to buy insurance. She deleted the sales and offer for insurance and replied to her friends.

While Jeffrey went to brush his teeth, she put on make-up and brushed her shoulder length hair. She twisted it into a braid to stay out of her way while she was at work and then called down the hall to see if Jeffery was waiting.

When she heard him clattering in his room, she called, "I need to leave now. Are you ready?"

He drifted in, juggling a box in his arms.

"What do you have?" Lauren asked.

"This is my old comic book collection. I'm going to read them again today. I made a schedule so I wouldn't be so bored. After I read, I'm going to draw some comics on the paper in the box. Then, I'll look up card tricks on my iPad and learn them. I might want to be a magician one day."

"It sounds good and should keep you busy."

"I wish Ruby had a dog. I could play with it. I wouldn't get bored then. Could we get a dog? I really want one."

"That's a big commitment, honey. Dogs take lots of care and you can't lose your temper when they make mistakes. Also, we're not home a lot during the day. The dog would be lonesome alone in the yard."

"I wouldn't get mad at him and he could stay inside with me and sleep on my bed at night. I'd take care of him and you wouldn't have to do anything."

"Dogs are expensive," Lauren countered. "They have vet visits and food for us to buy. When you are old enough to earn money, maybe we can get a dog."

"I can earn money now by doing jobs in the neighborhood."

She smiled at his confidence. "All right. Let me know when you get those jobs, and we'll talk about a dog."

He opened his mouth and then seemed to think better of it. He set down his box to pick up his coat and then hefted it into his arms again.

The bright sunshine had Lauren scrambling in her purse for her sunglasses. She found them and placed them on her face to filter out the bright light. Then, they hopped into the car and headed to Ruby's house.

When they arrived, Lauren expected Jeffrey to drag his feet about getting out. Usually, he dragged her along in his suffering by taking so long to get into the house that she had to worry about being late to work.

Today, he got right out and walked beside her to the door. As she glanced sideways, she was struck by how fast he was growing. In a short time, he would catch up to her height. Though his young years had been trying, they had passed. Nostalgia filled her at the fact that he was no longer a little boy. Jeffrey was growing up and there was no going back.

When she arrived at work, people were waiting for the store to open. There was a huge sale on printers and computers and Lauren knew the store was going to be a zoo all day. She slipped into the employee entrance on the side door and locked it behind her. Carol immediately enlisted her to help with product displays. Lauren wasn't going to get as much work done today as she had hoped. With the extra sales expected, she would be directing customers and filling in as an extra cashier.

Though she loved the Christmas season, the decorations, Jeffrey's anticipation about his presents, and, this year, going to church with the grandparents, it was a hard season at work. She could already see a line forming at the glass front doors and it was still twenty minutes until opening.

Inside the store, the employees scuttled around rechecking items in stock. They were running low on one of the printers and would have to call in for additional supplies before the sale ended tomorrow. Estimating from what they had sold yesterday, they would need at least twenty more. Lauren called it in and was assured they would have them by the afternoon. Lauren hoped, they could last until then.

When the doors opened at nine o'clock, folks streamed in for sale items, large, and small. The colorful Christmas wrap, and bows were hot items as well as the ceramic Christmas villages that Carol had managed to snag for the store. They hardly breathed until things slowed down a bit by noon.

Lauren took a lunch break in her office and prepared to work on the year-end books. She slogged through line item details before calling it quits at five o'clock. She wondered how Jeffrey had done with Ruby. Though he didn't like going there, Lauren wondered if he could manage to stay in the Boy's and Girl's Club. If she refused to let him try, it would send him the message that she didn't have confidence that he could change. She had to let him try even if she dreaded the embarrassment his possible failure would bring her.

CHAPTER NINE

Abby fixed Vic an evening meal of Salisbury steak and mashed potatoes. Though Vic wasn't picky and had never complained about the food, it was his favorite meal. The smell of the meat simmering on the stove brought him to the kitchen.

He sniffed. "Smells great."

Abby formed the last roll and set it on the pan. "The meat is almost done. I'm sticking these rolls in the oven. So, it will be about ten more minutes," she said.

"I must have dozed off in my chair. I didn't notice when you came in here," he said.

"You dozed for about two hours. I was only in there with you for a half-hour."

He peeked in the pot on the stove to see the green beans that would go with dinner and nodded in approval. "Where did you go?"

She smiled slyly. "Maybe I was wrapping someone's Christmas presents while he wasn't snooping around."

He raised a white brow. "You have a boyfriend, huh?"

"Yes. He's a young thing with lots more energy than you."

Vic chuckled. "Was he around this afternoon? I think he has a crush on you."

"As a grandmother, perhaps, and no, he wasn't around today. I think Lauren takes him to that sitter he doesn't like.

"You didn't like him too much a while back," Vic observed."

She began mashing the potatoes. A cloud of steam rose above them as she worked.

"That was before I knew him. I only saw how ill-behaved he was when he lost his temper. He hasn't done that once around us," she said.

Vic pulled out his chair and sat down. "No. He hasn't, even when he loses in a game. He loves playing chess with me and hasn't won once."

"He's doing chores for us too. He didn't ask to get paid until you offered to give him a bit for taking out the trash when he said he wanted to buy a gift for his mom."

"Don't forget he asked us to take him shopping," Vic reminded her.

"I'll call tonight when Lauren gets home and ask if we can take him tomorrow. Maybe we could pick him up early from the sitter, so we don't have to go in the evening."

Vick took a sip from the mug of amber ginger tea Abby had set on the table. "Good idea. I'm curious to meet the woman."

"If we weren't so old, I'd offer to watch Jeffrey for Lauren during the days he's off for his break. It would probably be too much for us now, though."

Abby scooped the creamy mashed potatoes into her blue Pennsylvania Dutch bowl that matched the plates on the table. Then she took the Salisbury steak from the pan and set both dishes on the table. The green beans went into a smaller matching bowl and the rolls on a pretty poinsettia Christmas plate.

Vic said grace and they dug into their meal. "This is food that will stick to your ribs on a cold night like this."

Abby took a bite and nodded. "Heavier food is always better in the winter. I don't feel like stews or chili in the summer. Making them heats up the kitchen too much, too."

After they finished the main course, they followed it with a slice of hot cherry pie for dessert. Then, they retired to the living room to their "his and hers" cozy armchairs. Though the love seat matched the green, blue and maroon flowered sofa, they rarely used it. Besides, their cozy nests in their chairs felt warmer in the winter. When a flannel lap blanket was added, it was warm, indeed. Since the chairs sat next to one another at the end of the sofa, they were still companionably close.

Abby read a cozy mystery while Vic was immersed in a political thriller. It was a while before Abby remembered to call Lauren. She took her phone from her pocket and punched in Lauren's number.

"It's Abby. I hope this isn't a bad time," she said when Lauren answered.

"No. Jeffrey just got off to bed. I'm sitting on the sofa and unwinding. It was a crazy day at work."

"End of the year wrap-up?"

Lauren sighed. "Yes. Also, I was pressed into service onto the sales floor for most of the morning. Carol is short-handed for the number of customers her sale produced."

"Wow. Maybe she can raise your salary."

Lauren smiled at the thought. "That would be nice. I know she has a lot of overhead and she does pay me fairly."

"That's good because you're worth it."

"Oh, that's sweet. Thank you."

She sounded so touched that Abby realized she probably had no one in her life to give her this sort of affirmation. Abby realized it would have been hard to raise her children without Vic's help. She still relied on him for many things. He was her go-to when anything was broken, for he was handy at repairing anything from toasters to furnaces. Even more than that, he was her emotional support. She couldn't imagine not having him here to ground her when her feelings got hurt by a friend or she failed at her efforts to learn a new craft.

"Anyway," Abby continued, "Vic and I would like to pick Jeffrey up tomorrow before you get home and take him shopping. He has a present he'd like to buy, and he wants it to be a surprise."

"That's kind, but I don't think he has much money. I wouldn't want you and Vic to give him any."

Don't worry, honey. Jeffrey has earned any money he's spending," Abby assured her.

"In that case, it would be wonderful for you to take him. He's been asking me, but it's hard for me to find time."

"It's our pleasure. Vic and I have lots of time."

Lauren had a catch in her voice when she answered, "He loves both of you."

"We love both of you, too," Abby said.

"Thank you for adopting us."

"Maybe we need you as much as you need us," Abby said.

With a catch in her voice, she said, "That's good to know."

When they'd said good-night, Abby told Vic, "I believe God sent those two into our lives to help us focus less on missing our kids and grandkids. I feel sorry for myself every year at Christmas that we don't have the girls nearby. I still miss them this year, yet not as much."

Vic stared over the top of his glasses to say, "I never thought we'd live so far apart and depend on twice a week calls to keep up with their lives."

Abby became pensive. "I miss how I haven't been able to do the things with Julie's kids that I did with her. I would like to have been a bigger part of their lives. Yet now we have a boy who needs grandparents and maybe we can do those things with him."

"We're about to do that tomorrow when we take him shopping. I hope his expectations aren't too high about how much he can buy," Vic said.

"We can help a little since it's for his mom."

Vic suppressed a smile. "A little, Abby, but not a lot. Kids have to learn the value of money."

"I said, a little."

She went back to the book she'd been reading. Vic watched her with a smile lingering on his lips. She was his lifelong love and they'd been blessed to grow old together.

The next morning, Abby drew the front curtains to see trees turned into white skeletons, ghostly silhouettes with ice on their branches. At eight in the morning, the sky was clear and blue without a cloud in sight. The bright sunshine cheered her and was a welcome relief from the days with heavy, gray, clouds. Better still, the forecast predicted above freezing temperatures in the afternoon. The roads should be okay for taking Jeffrey shopping.

Abby grabbed a mug of coffee and settled in her armchair in the living room. This was her sacred time when Vic was asleep to read her scriptures and pray. Now that she knew a few more neighbors, there were more folks to include in prayer. She had Jeffrey and Lauren and the sweet young woman, Krista, who lived next door. She had brought food when Abby had been sick with that dastardly virus. Last Sunday, she'd seen Krista at church with the young man across the street. Were they dating? Abby hadn't noticed them being outside together in the fall. Perhaps, their relationship was new and had recently developed. She prayed for God's care and sovereignty over their lives. Then she focused on her own children. It had been a concern for several years whether her girls had let their busy lifestyle push God out of their lives. With numerous competing demands on their time, life was busy. In this stage of life, God was often the first to go until a crisis brought Him to mind. She hoped this wasn't the case with Julie and Linda.

Her quiet time was interrupted when Vic appeared in the doorway. His white hair was rumpled, and his robe was askew. His eyes were bleary without his glasses. They had faded over time from sky blue to powder blue.

Abby pushed back annoyance at having her quiet time interrupted. He would want breakfast and she would have to clear away the dirty dishes and clean up the mess before she could read again. If Vic wanted to talk, it would be even longer. Also, she needed to make a trip to the grocery store for food for Christmas dinner. She wanted to make it especially special with Lauren and Jeffrey joining them.

There would be a Swedish tea ring for breakfast and lasagna with sprigs of parsley on top and homemade rolls. Homemade pecan pie would follow for dessert. To pull this off she needed nuts and several other ingredients from the store.

"Do you want eggs and toast?" Abby asked.

"Sure."

He pulled his robe tighter around him. "Brr. It's cold in here."

"You don't usually get up until after I've turned up the heat. By then, the house is warmer."

Vic rubbed a hand over his chin. "I know. I don't know what woke me, but I couldn't get back to sleep."

"You'll probably sleep during the day," Abby predicted.

"I probably will."

He followed her as she trod into the kitchen to fix their breakfast. She handed him a mug of coffee to sip while he waited.

When the eggs were nearly scrambled, she popped two pieces of toast into the toaster and poured orange juice while she waited for the toast to pop up.

When the toast was done, she buttered it and loaded the eggs onto two plates. She set one in front of Vic and took the other for herself.

After Vic said the breakfast prayer, they ate the meal. It was warm and filling on the cold winter morning.

When they finished Abby rinsed the plates and loaded them into the dishwasher. "Do you want anything else?" she asked Vic.

"Yes. I'd like to be twenty-five years old again and I'd like for it to be springtime and warm"

Abby sighed. "I might like the springtime but being twenty-five again sounds exhausting. Remember how busy we were?"

"Yes. I also remember how I had the energy to be busy instead of being tired all the time."

"We're like clocks winding down," she mused.

"I am, at least," Vic said. "You keep going better than I do. I'm going back to bed to rest a while until the house warms up more."

Abby wiped the table and said, "I'll read my scriptures and do a little cleaning, nothing noisy that will wake you."

"Who said I'll be sleeping?"

Abby cocked her head and gave him a knowing look. "You think you won't?"

Vic grinned at her. "I wouldn't bet on it."

After he'd trundled off, Abby returned to her chair and her scripture reading for the day. It came from John 1:14. "The Word became flesh and made his dwelling among us. We have seen his glory, the glory of the one and only Son, who came from the Father, full of grace and truth." RSV

She thought about the attributes of grace and truth and the beauty of the words. Though she felt she was often lacking, she longed to be full of both of them.

She checked on Vic to find him peacefully sleeping. It would do him good since they had an afternoon of shopping with Jeffrey. He was a child with energy. If Abby could bottle it and sell it, she would be rich.

Yesterday, she had determined that, today, she would give the small side-by-side refrigerator a good cleaning. She began by checking for any items that had expired. She tossed out the salad dressing and strawberry yogurt and a half-used carton of sour cream. By the time she finished wiping the interior of the refrigerator, Vic ambled into the room. He was dressed in loose fitting brown slacks a warm beige sweater.

"Did you get rested?" she asked.

"Yes. The house is warmer. The cold didn't use to bother me. Now it hurts my bones."

She nodded. "I know what you mean."

The house was old and somewhat drafty. She supposed the reason he spent so much time in his chair was that he felt comfortable under his warm lap blanket. He'd puttered around more in the fall, raking leaves, and repairing a broken part of their back fence. He always came in a little winded.

"We're going to have nice weather for getting out this afternoon," Abby said. "The high is going to be thirty-five with a clear sky. We won't have to worry about slipping on ice."

"Been about five years since the evening you fell on ice and broke your wrist," Vic said.

Abby shivered. "I remember. It was one of the scariest days of my life. I knew when my feet slipped that I couldn't break my fall. I put my hands down and hoped I'd end up with only a few bruises. Instead, I got a broken bone that put me out of commission for six weeks. You had to do a lot more around the house and I felt useless."

Vic enveloped her in a bear hug that hindered restocking the contents of the refrigerator. It had been a while since he'd hugged her like this, and it took her off guard. Her initial reaction of surprise faded into simply enjoying the comfort of his arms. The food could wait

After a few more moments, he released her.

"What time are we picking up the boy?" he asked.

"Lauren told the sitter we'd be there at three-thirty."

"After we finish shopping, we could bring him over here until his mom gets home. I wouldn't mind a game or two of checkers with him."

"You're enjoying having a boy, aren't you?" Abby asked.

Vic grinned. "I guess I am."

They left at three o'clock for the twenty-minute drive to Ruby's house. They found it on a tree- lined street across town. The only pretty thing about the property was the towering pine in the center of the yard. Sparse grass lay in scattered patches in the yard. The house sat behind a railed front porch. Lime green paint peeled on all the trim.

They walked the L-shaped sidewalk to the front of the house. Two seventies-era window frames also needed painting. Vic had never let any house he'd owned get in this bad of shape.

Abby said, "If she had a husband to help her, maybe things would look better. Lauren said Ruby's husband left her a few years ago for someone else. Perhaps she lacks the funds or incentive to improve the house."

Vic rang the dangling doorbell and Ruby answered the door. She wasn't what he expected.

She peered unsmilingly at them. Her thick, black eyeliner and frizzled blond hair gave her a hardened appearance. Instead of inviting them inside, she blocked Jeffrey's path out of the house.

"You sure you got all the electronic stuff you brought?" she asked him.

"I'm sure. It was just my iPad today. "

"You had some books, too."

Jeffrey patted the blue backpack he'd slung over his shoulder. "They're in here."

"Okay. I'm having company and I don't want to pick up."

From what Vic could see of her living room, it didn't look like she ever picked up.

Ruby finally stepped aside. "I hope he behaves for you," she said as Jeffrey left the house.

"Don't let him get away with anything," she warned Vic and Abby. "He can be hard to manage."

"We'll be fine," Vic assured her as she abruptly shut the door.

Jeffrey was already at the car. "Thank you for picking me up. I get so bored with Ruby. There's nothing to do. Mom says I can try Boys and Girls Club after Christmas if I don't lose my temper."

"We know you can do it," Abby said.

"Thanks. I'm really going to try."

Afternoon traffic grew heavier as they headed to the discount store where Jeffrey wanted to buy his mother a present. The late afternoon sun rested low in the sky in a glow of fiery red.

In the last half hour, the temperature dropped ten degrees. The car heater thrummed out a continuous stream of warm air. When the windows began to steam-up, Vic turned on the defroster. "It's going to be a cold one tonight," he said.

Jeffrey stared out the sedan's back seat window. Along the street, garlands wrapped the light poles. Trees in the esplanade wore shiny red and white balls that sparkled in the fading light. Plate glass windows on the storefronts displayed decals of Santa and Christmas trees. Behind the windows, mannequins wore colorful winter outfits of red and green and glittery gold. Some of the stores displayed the latest toys that were advertised over and again on television.

Vic pulled into the parking lot of the discount store and joined a crawling line of cars trolling the lot to find a parking place. In the back of the lot, a spot opened, and Vic wheeled the sedan into it. It would be a long, cold walk up to the store.

Trees planted at the end of the parking rows cast bony shadows on the crosswalk that led to the store. Abby's cheeks burned from the cold and Vic breathed heavily by the time they got to the automatic doors.

Inside, the store was aglow with decorated trees for sale and electronic toys. Secular Christmas music played to put them in the mood to shop. Jeffrey had asked his mom for a video game update and a dinosaur model kit. Abby knew something else he would like. Since he liked drawing, she and Vic had purchased him an art kit for Christmas. They couldn't wait to surprise him with it on Christmas morning.

They scanned the aisle sign information to the tune of "Rocking Around the Christmas Tree". When they found the marking for small appliances, they were off in search of a toaster. Jeffrey peered at each model and read the prices.

"This one makes four pieces at once. We don't need that much," he said. "Besides, it costs twenty-five bucks."

"I remember when it would have cost five bucks," Vic said.

"That was a long time ago," Abby said.

She picked up a boxed model and read what it could do. "Look, Jeffrey. This one is seventeen dollars."

Jeffrey's expression fell. "I only have fifteen dollars."

"Are you taking our trash out next week and bringing the can back to the house?" Vic asked.

Jeffrey raised a brow. "Sure."

"We'll pay the difference for the toaster as an advance for next week," Vic said.

Jeffrey brightened. "Really? Hey, thanks. I'll take the trash out and sweep the back porch. I'll do whatever else you want me to do."

"Thank you, honey," Abby said. "Having you empty out our inside trash and take the big can out each week helps a lot."

Jeffrey beamed. "Mom will be happy with this."

"Let's buy it," Vic said.

They made their way through the crowd of shoppers who squeezed past one another down the aisles and jostled for positions at the clothing racks. Carts filled with toys, clothing, and electronics presented obstacle paths that had the threesome veering as they swerved to reach the check out.

The lines were all full, and it took ten minutes before it was their turn. Jeffrey pulled from his pocket the money he'd earned, and Vic supplied the rest. They had no worries he'd be good for his debt. He thrived on being helpful to them.

They left the store as the sun lost the battle for dominion of the sky and became a shade of her former self. She began to bow out to make way for the prince of the night sky. In the morning, the roles would be reversed in a graceful relinquishment of dominance.

They scurried through the parking lot in a stiff, cold, breeze and reached the shelter of the car. They hopped inside and Vic started the engine. Moments later, the heater blew out blessed warmth that drained the chill from their bones.

As they drove from the lot, Jeffrey touched his nose to the window. "Wow. It's cold," he said.

"Yes, it is, "Vic said. He glanced at Abby before returning his attention to the road. "The first time I met you, your cheeks were rosy from the cold air."

"I remember that like it was yesterday."

"What was she doing that made her so cold?" Jeffrey asked.

Vic smiled at the memory. "She was ice skating. It was early December, and the pond was frozen. I was never a good skater. Grandma was wonderful. She could do spins and figure eights like nothing you ever saw."

Abby's eyes shone as she looked at Vic. "You're exaggerating."

"You were the prettiest thing I'd ever seen."

"Did you skate in the Olympics?" Jeffrey asked.

Abby gave a hearty laugh. "Goodness, no. I wasn't that good."

"I bet you were great. Would you teach me?" Jeffrey asked.

"I'd love to. We'll have to go to the rink. The pond isn't frozen yet this year."

"Could we go next week?"

"I think we could. You'll have to ask your mom, though."

"I'll ask her tonight."

"Are you planning on skating?" Vic asked. "You haven't done it in years. I don't want you getting hurt."

"You never lose it. Besides, I'll be careful."

"I'm going along to keep an eye on you," Vic said.

"Will you skate?" Jeffrey asked Vic.

"Not a chance. I lose my balance walking across the living room."

"Maybe I'll be an Olympic skater," Jeffrey said.

Abby smiled at Jeffrey. "You never know."

When they reached the cul-de-sac, it gave Abby a warm feeling to see lights in the windows. Her neighbors were home, snug and secure. The lights brought back recollections of her girlhood home. In the winter, when she was young, her mother drove her home in the late afternoons after her piano lesson each week. The front windows would be lit, and her father would be in the kitchen making them grilled cheese sandwiches and hot soup. The memory made her feel warm inside.

They pulled up to Jeffrey's house and he asked, "Will you be my grandparents? I know it wouldn't be a legal kind of real, but I never see my real grandparents. My grandpa died before I knew him, and my Grandma is always traveling with her new husband. She calls my mom sometimes and makes her sad."

Abby began to explain how Jeffrey should understand that his grandparents must love him very much and there was probably a good reason they couldn't visit often. Vic cut her off and said, "We'd be honored to be your grandparents. You can call us Grandma and Grandpa anytime you like."

"Thanks." Jeffrey's eyes shone as he got out of the car.

When they got home, Abby asked, "What was the reason you interrupted me like that. We don't want Jeffrey to think his grandparents don't love him."

Vic looked her in the eyes. "Jeffrey needs grandparents who are with him right now. The reason his grandparents can't be around doesn't matter right now. He doesn't feel loved by them. If it helps him to think of us as his grandparents, we should accept."

Abby's eyes welled with tears. "He should understand that sometimes grandparents can't be with him, even if they want to."

Vic enveloped her in a hug. "You're thinking of us. I understand how you feel. Still, we're not like Jeffrey's grandparents. We travel to see the kids twice a year and we talk with them every week. We try. Jeffrey's knows his grandparents could visit a lot more and that they make other choices."

He tipped Abby's face to look up at him. "You don't mind Jeffrey thinking of us as grandparents, do you?"

"Of course not. I've become fond of him. I only wish we could have ours with us, too."

Vic kissed her forehead. "I understand. I wish ours could be with us, too. Still, let's take what we can get, and we'll see the other two in the spring."

"We'll make a video call with the kids on Christmas," Abby said. "All of our grandkids can meet."

"We'll have a happy Christmas with Lauren and Jeffrey," Vic said.

Abby nodded. "Yes. We will. There are so many things I still need to get done. I should get to it."

Vic shook his head. "Not tonight. You have a date."

"To do what?" Abby asked.

Vic grinned. "You'll see."

CHAPTER TEN

Krista's mouth fell open when her mom balked at having Trent's parents over on Christmas Day. She'd always been hospitable, so it wasn't at all like her.

"Why won't it work?" Krista asked.

"I'm too embarrassed to tell you."

"I think you'd better since I've already invited them," Krista said.

"Are you sure we can't forget the whole thing?" her mom asked.

"No, Mom. We can't"

"All right, but it's not pretty."

After a hesitation, Doris said, "We were in a quilting club together when we first moved here. There was a show and sale at the Civic Center. During the show, a woman came up to me and expressed a lot of interest in my quilt. Right when I thought I had her sold, Amanda came and stole her away. Then, I saw the woman walking out with one of Amanda's quilts. I was steamed and I marched over and told Amanda what I thought about what she'd done."

Kristy was flummoxed until her mom continued.

Doris said, "She nicely explained to me that the woman was her sister, and the quilt was promised to one of her sister's kids. I felt about two inches tall when I apologized and slunk away. I didn't go back to the club because I couldn't face her again. I still can't."

"I understand how you feel, but you're going to have to face her. I won't come if you don't."

Her mother's voice broke. This is just terrible. Christmas is ruined."

"Your embarrassment with her happened years ago. I doubt she ever thinks about it. Even if she does, she's too nice to bring it up."

"I know. I'm not nice at all."

"You're very nice. Still, I'm not willing to give this up. I really like Trent."

Doris' tone changed. "This might be serious, then?"

"It's still early, but it might be."

"Oh my, in that case, I'll do it. It's going to be hard."

Now that she'd agreed, Krista saw amusement in the situation. She tried to imagine her mom storming over to confront Amanda and her chagrin when she learned the truth. No one could accuse Mom of holding back her thoughts.

"Thanks, Mom. It will go well. You're a gracious hostess. Amanda's probably forgotten all about the quilt confrontation."

"I hope so. Yet, I doubt it. I wouldn't have forgotten."

She was telling the truth. Doris remembered every social situation, good or bad. Perhaps there was a way to ease her through the discomfort. To do so, Krista determined to come up with a solution. She owed it to her mom since she was the one insisting on bringing the embarrassment to Mom's own house.

She toyed with the idea of giving Amanda a heads-up about the Civic Center confrontation. Yet, if she admitted how embarrassed her mom still felt, Amanda might change her plans about coming. Then, Trent would stay with Amanda and Krista would have to decide between spending Christmas with her parents or with Trent. Before she took any action, she should probably give it some thought.

She padded into her bedroom to slip into a gown and watch television until she got sleepy. She wouldn't stay up too late because she worked a seven to five o'clock shift tomorrow. It was a killer. Yet it allowed her to work a four-day week. She loved having three days off and used one to do housework, the next for shopping and running errands. She had Sundays completely off.

Her thoughts drifted to Trent. She would see him tomorrow night. It would be a good time to tell him that her mom wanted to apologize and wasn't sure how to do it. Maybe Trent would have a suggestion.

She propped her sock feet on the coffee table and flipped through the channels. She found a clean Christmas romance on a channel that ran them every evening and she settled on the couch with a fuzzy fleece blanket her grandma had given her on her birthday. It brought back happy memories of Christmas with Grandma. They baked sugar cookies during the week before Christmas, iced them with colored frosting and sprinkles, and passed them out to the neighbors. She'd made the recipe once after her grandma passed away. It made her so sad she froze the dough and finally had to throw it away.

When the movie was half-over, she turned it off and went to bed. It was chilly in the house and the down comforter felt good. She fell asleep in less than five minutes.

The next day she parked at the staff lot of the regional hospital and hurried through the frigid morning air to the entrance. She greeted the receptionist before she continued along the shiny hallway tile to her job in the operating room.

They had two scheduled surgeries and an emergency appendectomy. After a late lunch in the cafeteria, she assisted in a three-hour surgery before completing paperwork and going off-duty. She left the hospital at five-thirty for the trip home. With a week and a half left until Christmas, shoppers were out in force. Traffic backed up over of quarter of a mile to get to the mall. Since there wasn't a better route, Krista listened to Christmas music and tried to be patient. All she wanted was to get home to a quick supper and a warm bath.

When she finally pulled into her garage, her rumbling stomach sent her straight into the kitchen. She heated frozen taquitos and grabbed a packaged green salad from the refrigerator. Ten minutes later, dinner was served.

She enjoyed the quiet of her simple kitchen and a chance to relax after a day on her feet.

As she cleared away the dishes, her cell phone rang. Trent was calling.

"Hi," he said. "How was your day?"

"Busy. A lot of people want to get their surgeries done before Christmas."

"I bet you're tired," he said.

Hearing his voice perked her up. "I am. I'm glad you called, though."

"I thought about you all day today," he said.

"That's sweet. I hope they were good thoughts."

"All good," he assured her. "I'm looking forward to Christmas. I thought I might see you sooner, though. You're off Thursday night, right?"

"Yes. What did you have in mind?"

"The Civic Center is having a Christmas Concert featuring a local orchestra. Would you like to go?"

"I would love to go. Hearing it on the radio isn't the same as hearing it live."

She imagined sitting next to him, his warm shoulder against her as she soaked in the beautiful songs she'd known since childhood and played in piano recitals. She could still hear her mom singing along from another part of the house as Krista practiced. She brought her thoughts back when Trent asked, "Could you be ready by six? We could go to dinner and then hear the concert.

"I can be ready. In fact, I can't wait."

"Good. It won't take long to pick you up."

Krista heard the humor in this voice, and replied, "It certainly won't, will it neighbor."

Her confidence grew when he asked, "Would you like to help me take Angel for a walk on a day you're off? "

Happy warmth spread within her. "I would love to. I'm off on Thursday."

"Thursday, it is"

She hesitated a moment yet couldn't deny what her heart told her to say. "We really want you and your mom to come for Christmas. There's something you should know, though. My mom feels bad about an incident that happened when we were new here. She misunderstood a situation and accused your mom of luring a customer away at a quilt fair. My mom felt really awful about it and is still embarrassed about what she did. I'm sure your mom has put it behind her, and we really want you two to come. "Could you tell your mom how sorry mine still is and ask if she wants to come over?"

"Sure, but I can tell you now that it won't bother her to come."

"I hope you're right because I want to spend Christmas with you."

Voice husky, he replied. "Not more than I want to spend it with you."

"Then let's hope your mom is okay with mine," Krista said.

"She will be. Even if not, I'd still spend Christmas with you?"

Like water down a pipe, a surge of happiness shot through Krista's veins. I decided the same thing," she said.

"So now it's up to them," Trent said. "I'll see you Thursday for a walk. About five o'clock?"

"Perfect."

When they hung up, Krista clutched the phone for a few moments, feeling as though he was still there. Then she chuckled. He was only two houses down from her and not across town. It gave her a warm feeling to have him so close.

Now she would enjoy a warm bath. She scooped a fresh set of blue flannel pajamas from the closet and secured them on the hook on the back of the bathroom door. She took off her socks and threw them into the dirty clothes hamper built into the wall under the cabinet. She ran her toes in the fluffy blue bath rug while she started the water running into the tub.

When it was full and warm, she slid into the water and let it ease her tired muscles.

On Thursday, she bundled into her insulated coat and met Trent. Angel danced with excitement to see Krista, who knelt to pet her.

"I've missed you, too," Krista said.

"If I hunker down and shake, will you say you've missed me?" Trent asked.

"Would you?" Krista cocked her head, daring him.

"No. I have a little more dignity than my dog."

"I missed you both," Krista said.

He gazed into her eyes as a smile graced his charming face. "Have I told you you're beautiful?"

Her heartbeat quickened from his compliment.

"Thank you.

He smiled at her. "I'm sure it's not the first time you've heard it. You make me feel like cold winter days are warm and sunny."

"That's so sweet," she said. "I feel the same way about you."

He cupped her chin and kissed her gently, yet briefly. They broke it off when Angel scratched at their legs and danced around them in anticipation of her walk. Krista smiled down at her.

"Your girlfriend is jealous."

Trent chuckled. "I can tell."

They set off down the sidewalk with Trent holding Angel's leash as she walked on the outside with Trent and Krista walking together. Dusk was descending. It would give way to darkness before they finished the walk. They rounded a corner and the streetlights flickered on. Krista could see Trent's profile in the soft glow of the light. His dark hair shone in a raven glow. The memory of his loving gaze and firm lips that she had recently tasted made her smile.

Above them, the moon hung like a crescent in the velvet December sky. Stars glittered like a million diamonds. Krista's breath blew smoke into the frigid air. She didn't care that it was cold or if her feet hurt from standing on them all day. If it turned out that she and Trent spent a lifetime together, she wanted to remember this evening forever. She thought that she, Trent, and Angel made a perfect family.

They rounded the cul-de-sac and stopped at her house. She said, "I haven't straightened in a couple of days but you're welcome to come in."

He tightened Angel's leash as she pulled to go home. "Do you have time to grab something to eat? I could take Angel home and come back for you."

Her choice was easy. She could eat a cold sandwich and soup alone or have supper with Trent.

"I'd love to," she said.

Angel tugged harder.

Trent said, "Let me take this little beast home and feed her before she eats my leg. I'll be right back."

"No hurry," Krista said. "Take care of her while I get ready. It won't take me long."

Krista changed out of her work clothes and into a warm cashmere sweater, baby blue and chinchilla soft. She pulled on gray slacks and low boots. Moments later, Trent rang the bell.

"Did I give you time?" he asked.

She nodded. "I just need my coat."

She pulled her full-length insulated coat from the closet and Trent helped her into it. Extracting sleek black gloves from a pocket, she slipped her hands into them.

Smiling at Trent, she said, "Now I'm ready."

He'd parked in her driveway. It was a short walk to the car that was already warming. Krista belted into the seat beside him and he asked, "What sounds good? We'll go wherever you like."

Krista didn't have to think long. "A simple Italian place would be great if it's not fancy."

He backed from the driveway and said, "I know just where to go."

Krista stopped shivering as the inside of the car warmed, creating a cozy cocoon. Though her stomach pleaded for a meal, she would be content to sit for hours in the cozy car with Trent sat beside her, making her feel like a princess in a fairy tale.

Nonetheless, they reached the restaurant on Center Street. The lit sign in front boasted in red letters that Mama Mia's had the best Italian food in the state.

Her mouth watered at the thought of warm sauce full of Italian spices, melted cheese, and tender noodles. Though she'd learned to make acceptable lasagna, it never tasted as good as ones from the best Italian restaurants.

The brick building was built in a cozy cottage style, warm and homey as soon as they walked in. A young woman with dark hair and striking green eyes greeted them from behind a high desk and asked if there were two for dinner.

"Yes." Krista smiled back at the girl.

She picked up two menus and stepped from behind the desk, "This way, please."

They entered the dining room that had a beamed ceiling and an electric fireplace with a perpetual crackling log at the far end. Tables filled the center of the rectangular room while booths lined the walls. Above the booths were black and white photos of vineyards and stone houses set along cobblestone streets. Perhaps they were the ancestral homes of the owners of the restaurant.

When the hostess asked Krista which she would prefer, Krista chose the privacy of a booth. She slid into one side and Trent sat across from her. "Did the family come from Italy," she asked.

"The parents, yes. I believe the kids were all born here."

"Fascinating. Italy is on my bucket list to visit someday," she said.

"You'd love it. Rome is a typical big city. The countryside is slowed-down and friendly. Folks in the small towns love to visit with travelers. They'll show you their vineyards and invite you to dinner. I accompanied my mom and her friend on a trip there when Mom turned fifty. We all had a great time. Her friend had relatives in one of the towns. We all rode bikes out to the countryside and had a picnic. Afterwards, we went back into town for gelato. It was amazing. If they had it here, I'd get you some, but they don't. They have a great tiramisu."

"If you don't slow down, I won't be able to waddle out of here."

Trent grinned at her. "You won't leave hungry. That's for sure."

Moments later, a young waitress brought their water. "My name is Maria. I'll be serving you today. Do you need a few more minutes to look over the menu?"

Maria looked a great deal like the young lady who had greeted them.

"Are you sisters?" Krista asked, nodding toward the girl at the entrance.

"We are. Our parents own the restaurant. Two of my brothers are working in the kitchen tonight. There are six kids and all of us have worked here."

"That must have made you a close family," Krista said.

"The girl nodded. "We are. We're normal, too, though. We have our disagreements. In an Italian family, they are loud."

Trent and Krista laughed.

"I can only imagine," Krista said, "I'm an only child and I always wanted a sister."

"I have three of them."

"You're lucky," Krista said.

Maria smiled. "Yes. I am."

The dark-haired beauty took their orders and returned to the kitchen to place them. She returned with bread sticks and garden salads.

"Your dinners will be out soon."

With that promise, she scurried to a new family of guests.

Krista limited herself to one breadstick and half of her salad. She knew from experience that if she ate more, she wouldn't have room for dinner.

While they waited for their food, Trent asked, "What do you see yourself doing five years from now?"

She didn't have to think about it. "I like nursing, but I'd like to quit for a while and raise a family."

"A big one like our waitress here?" His grin was mischievous.

Krista shook her head. "I was thinking two or three. It's nice to have a sibling, right?"

Trent rubbed the top of his arm. "Nice when they're not beating you up."

Krista fixed him with a stare. "You were always the victim, right?"

Trent raised his brows. "Of course."

Their dinners arrived and Maria put chicken Parmesan in front of Krista and shrimp Alfredo in front of Trent. Trent offered a blessing and they dug in. Krista fell in love at first bite. "This is the best I've ever had."

Trent nodded in agreement. "This is, hands down, my favorite place."

"How did you discover it?" she asked.

"High school prom. A group of us went together and I fell in love with this place. Not so much with my date. She fell for the guy who was dating her best friend."

"Did they get married and live happily ever after?" Krista asked.

"No. They broke up during their first year of college."

Krista speared a bite of steamed broccoli. "That's too bad."

"Maybe not. I never thought they were right for each other."

She wanted to ask if she and Trent were right for each other? However, that might imply she was expecting his commitment. It was too soon for that.

He surprised her by saying, "She wasn't like you. I'd be a fool to let you get away."

He set down his fork and looked into her eyes. She read deep yearning in his searching gaze.

"How do you feel about me? I need a heads up if you don't feel for me what I feel for you. Am I going to get my heart broken?"

Joy took wings inside her. "I don't think so."

He heaved a sigh. "That's a relief. I couldn't eat another bite until I knew the answer."

"Thank you for having the courage to ask. I had the same question."

He cocked his head to study her. "How could you doubt? Any man would be crazy not to fall for you."

"I'm glad you feel that way. I dated in college, yet never met the right person. Since then, I haven't dated much at all. A friend set me up on a blind date a couple of months ago with a business partner in a local firm. It was a disaster. He was totally stuck on himself and how valuable he was to the company."

"He was probably trying to impress you."

"It didn't work."

He grinned, mischief gleaming in his eyes. "Have I ever told you how important I am to my business?"

She rolled her eyes. "You're the owner. It wouldn't exist without you."

"It would if I sold it."

The notion startled her. "Are you thinking of selling?"

"No. I was just making a point."

She suppressed a smile as she scowled at him. "You're teasing me."

"Yep. You're too good of a sport to mind."

"You've never played a game of tennis against me. I was on the high school tennis team. I moped for days if we lost."

"It wasn't your fault if the team lost."

She nodded. "Sometimes it was."

He shook his head. "Naw. Still, I accept the challenge."

She searched his face. "You've played before, haven't you?"

"All through college. All state. It's interesting we have the same taste in a sport."

"Yes interesting." Krista wished the cold didn't make her reluctant to challenge him right away. "We can play some matches when it warms up a little. I won't even be a bad sport if I lose."

"That's good to know."

She smiled sweetly. "However, I might tie your shoelaces together when you're not looking."

He chuckled at her threat. "Remind me to wear Velcro."

"Never mind, then,"

He took her hand. Becoming serious, he said, "I love your sense of humor. There's no one I'd rather spend time with. You've become my best friend."

Her pulse quickened at his touch. "I feel the same way."

"Would you like dessert?" he asked.

"No. I'm full."

"Then let's go home so I can kiss you at your door."

She softly squeezed his hand. "Maybe I'll invite you in and you can kiss me during a romantic movie."

"Let's not wait." He released her hand and motioned the waitress for the check.

They walked to the car with his arm around her shoulders. Her anticipation of the rest of the evening made Krista feel giddy. God had blessed her with a man who had been right under her nose, a neighbor, and now, a handsome boyfriend.

CHAPTER ELEVEN

Trent's mom, Amanda, spent a whole morning praying about what to say to put Doris at ease. It had been years since the incident with the quilt. Amanda had forgotten about it a few days after it happened. Too bad Doris carried the embarrassment after all these years. For the sake of the kids, it was necessary for her to put it aside. Trent would feel guilty foregoing Christmas with his mom. This would put Krista in the position of choosing, which was both unfair and unnecessary.

She turned on the phone and put in the number Krista had given Trent.

When Doris answered, Amanda said, "Hi, I'm Amanda Dryden, Trent's Mom. I've fallen in love with your daughter. She is such a precious girl and I've never seen Trent so happy. It's been years since we've seen each other. How have you been?"

Amanda heard breathlessness in Doris's voice when she answered. "I've been fine. Nothing to complain about. How about you?"

"Life has been good. Trent and his brother spoil me. Parker moved three hours away a couple of years ago. I still see him on holidays and sometimes he comes on a weekend to visit. Of course, it will never be the same without their dad."

"I'm sorry. That must be hard."

"It will be hard unless I can spend Christmas with you. Trent told me about your gracious invitation, and I would like to accept."

Doris stammered. "Thank you for forgiving my blunder over the quilt."

Amanda waved her hand, even though Doris couldn't see her. "That was so long ago it doesn't even count. You forget all about it, okay?"

"I can do that and I'm happy you're going to be here."

"Me, too. May I bring cinnamon rolls or a breakfast casserole?"

"A casserole would be lovely. Thank you."

"Thank you for having me come."

"It is truly my pleasure and you have lifted a weight off my shoulders."

When they hung up, Amanda was pleased with the conversation and couldn't wait to tell Trent. When she called the business, one of the workers said he wasn't in. She left a message on his cell phone. He would be pleased that the situation was handled, and he and Krista would be together on Christmas Day.

Trent got the message during lunch break when he checked his calls. He was sitting in his cubbyhole in the portable he used to meet clients and do bookwork. He knew Krista would be at work, so he left her a text. Her anticipation of their first Christmas together was making it hard for him to concentrate on finalizing plans for a large home they were building on the mesa. The project was a four-thousand-foot brick colonial with an indoor pool and outdoor tennis court. It afforded a view of snow-capped mountains that would be visible on the right from the expansive front window. Below, lay the view of the rolling hills of their town.

It had been foremost in his thoughts until he met Krista.

Now, what to get her for Christmas burned in his thoughts. It should be something special that she should treasure. His desire to buy an engagement ring was strong though it was too soon to ask. Another kind of jewelry would have to do for now. Perhaps a necklace with a precious stone would be nice. He promised himself he would shop that afternoon.

Time zipped by while he checked payments to their accountant. He had a project he needed to check, and then, he could run to the jewelers.

When he finally got free of the accounts, he headed out of the building and into a blustery breeze. Light snowflakes landed on his lashes on the trek to his car. Low gray clouds looked as though there would be more where this had come. Flakes on the windshield melted as soon as they landed. The roads were clear. No need to worry about ice.

Christmas shopping had put dozens of cars on the roads and the mall parking lot looked like a bejeweled blanket of colorful cars. He was glad he wasn't headed there, though the jewelry store would likely be crowded as well.

The remodel was coming along on schedule. The family was living in the back of the house while the dining room, kitchen, and living room were being reworked. Trent inspected the work so far and found a flaw in the kitchen.

Trent told the young laborer. "Jake, your under-floor isn't level at this spot."

He pointed to an area of boards. "This will cause the tile to crack. You'll have to fill it and re-lay it."

The young man turned his head and studied his work. Do you mean there?"

Trent swept his hand over a yard breadth. "Re-do all of this part. Use your level."

Jake heaved a sigh and Trent lay a hand on his shoulder. "You'll get it."

He checked the hard floor in the living room and found it nicely laid. It required only stain and sealant. Of course, they had been laid by Rick, a seasoned employee who was out with the flu. They would cope until he got back.

His next stop was the jewelry store on 5th and Tucker. It was nestled in a small shopping center with a drugstore and cafeteria. He parked in the lot and headed to the store with windows decorated with decals of poinsettia blooms. Inside, the display cases were draped with fake greenery. A ceramic Santa in a sleigh pulled by his reindeer sat atop the cash register.

As he perused the cases, a woman with light brown hair colored with muted streaks of blond approached. She wore a smile that looked cultivated from long practice. She greeted him with, "What can I show you today, sir?"

"I'm looking for a nice necklace for my girlfriend."

The saleswoman responded with, "We have quite a good selection of necklaces if you'll step this way."

A woman beside them at a case of rings said, "How sweet. What a lucky girl."

Not knowing what to say, Trent thanked her and followed the saleswoman to the necklaces.

"These are our highest quality items. You can't go wrong here."

She was right. They were lovely items. There were gold chains in various thickness, gold and silver crosses, birthstone settings, and a silver chain and heart with a red onyx in the center of the heart. What would she like best? The choice was going to be difficult. As he imagined Krista in each one of them, he realized she would look lovely in anything in the case.

She wore a gold watch, so he narrowed the choices to a woven gold chain or a plain gold chain with golden flower petals and pearls inlaid in the center.

To help him in his choice, the saleswoman asked, "What sort of jewels does she wear?"

He thought, and then replied, "I've seen her in a gold cross and in a chain with blue tear drop beads. That's all I can remember."

"It sounds like she would like either of these."

The price for either necklace was nearly the same. Trent hesitated a moment and then went with his instincts. "I'll take the petals with pearls."

The lady smiled. "It's a good choice, sir. I'm sure she'll love it. Shall I wrap it?"

"Yes. Please do."

She returned with a small box in blue foil wrap and a red bow.

Elegant, Trent thought. He left the store feeling pleased with his purchase

CHAPTER TWELVE

Abby hummed as she wrapped the art set they had bought for Jeffrey. Lauren had insisted they shouldn't get him a gift and Abby had been adamant that it would make Vic and her happy to get Jeffrey something he would like. Vic had the idea to buy him a set of comic books, so Abby wrapped those, also, and put them in the pile. They had also bought Lauren a gift card to the discount store down the street. There would surely be something she needed there.

When she finished wrapping, she set the presents under the tree with the four she and Vic had bought each other. On years when their girls couldn't come for Christmas, Abby shipped their gifts, leaving it looking bare under the tree. Jeffrey's two gifts made it look better. Abby looked forward to watching him open them.

She had plans today to make cookies for each neighbor on the block. Lauren and Jeffrey were dear to her. The young woman in the house to her right had wanted to help when Abby had been sick. Abby would take some to her and try to learn if she was dating the young man who lived to the right of Lauren and Jeffrey. Bringing cookies would be a good way to meet him.

She busied herself in the kitchen creaming butter and sugar. She knew the old recipe by heart. Vic had taken Jeffrey with him to get an oil change for the car. If the shop wasn't too busy, they should be back soon.

The light snow that had fallen last night had melted. Her view of the back yard revealed sunlight spilling from a clear blue sky. Snow was forecast again by morning. Abby hoped it would be a light dusting that didn't' stick. She already looked forward to the warmer weather that usually began in April. As fast as time flew these days, it would be here before she knew it.

When her boys returned, she had ham sandwiches made and cookies cooling on the racks. Jeffrey eyed the cookies. "Are those for now?"

"You and Grandpa may each have three. The rest are to share."

"All right!"

"Eat your lunch first," Abby told him.

"All right."

When they'd eaten the sandwiches and sliced apple, Abby brought them each three cookies. After eating two Vic said, "I'm not hungry enough for this last one. Know anybody who'd want it?"

"I do." Jeffrey was quick to answer.

"Here you go." Vic slid it over to him.

"Grandma makes the best cookies ever. They're better than the ones in the packages Mom buys."

"Much better," Vic agreed.

"Will we have time to play chess today?" Jeffrey asked Vic.

"That depends on whether Grandma needs us for anything.".

"I thought it would be nice if we vacuumed your mom's floors. I'm sure she is extra busy right now," Abby told Jeffrey.

"Can we do it now? I want to have time for chess."

Abby smiled at his response. He had yet to balk when she told him what they needed to do."

"You use your mom's vacuum and I'll take mine. It will go faster that way."

Abby's vacuum was light and fit easily into the car. They drove to Jeffrey's house and parked in the driveway. Abby had a key to the door in case they needed to get in.

While Jeffrey vacuumed the bedrooms, bathrooms, and hall, Abby did the living room, dining room, and kitchen. It took them less than an hour to get finished.

"We still have time for chess, right?" Jeffrey asked Vic.

"At least two games," Vic answered."

Abby shook her head as Jeffrey ran to the hall closet. She'd never understand the strategy of chess. She'd given up playing with Vic soon after they were married. However, he still loved the game.

Two hours later, they were still playing when Lauren rang the bell.

"Was he good?" she asked.

She was finally sounding a little less nervous when she asked the question each day.

"He was fine. Good as gold," Abby said.

"Wonderful. Tomorrow he won't be here in the afternoon. He has an appointment with his doctor at 2:00 and I'm taking off what's left of the afternoon."

"That's fine. If you do need us, we'll be glad to have him Abby assured her."

"Thank you. You two are lifesavers"

"You are welcome. We love having Jeffrey here."

"Except he's getting too close at beating me at chess," Vic said.

The card table between their two chairs held the chess game. Jeffrey looked at his mom and said, "Do we have to go? We haven't finished the game."

"We can finish it in the morning," Vic said. "Your mom has had a long day and needs a man's help tonight, and you're that man."

Jeffrey rose from the game. "That's right. Tell me what you need help with Mom."

Dumbfounded, Lauren smiled at Vic, and then told Jeffrey, "I've got a few groceries in the car. You can bring those in."

"Okay. Bye Grandpa. Bye Grandma. I'll see you in the morning."

Lauren shot them a grateful look and then left.

Vic hoisted himself out of his chair and stood up. "I think my feet have gone to sleep," he complained as he sank onto the sofa.

"You've been sitting too long. The doctor said to keep your circulation moving."

"I know. I'd be out taking a walk but it's too cold."

"At least walk around the house a little more," Abby said. She worried that Vic was too sedentary.

"I will," he said.

Yet he never did.

Jeffrey bounced in the next morning to finish the chess game. Abby was up, yet Vic was still in bed. When Jeffrey didn't see him, he repeated what Abby had told him.

"I know. Grandpa doesn't like cold mornings and stays in bed awhile to stay warm."

"That's right. He'll be out soon. Would you like some breakfast? I'm making scrambled eggs."

Jeffrey frowned. "Mom made me eat some cereal at home so I wouldn't eat up all your food."

"I have plenty of eggs. I'll make you a batch."

Jeffrey grinned. "Thanks."

They were in the middle of eating Abby's creamy scrambled eggs when Vic appeared already dressed in brown slacks and a warm, checkered, flannel shirt with buttons up the front.

Jeffrey pointed to the red and white checkered squares on Vic's shirt and said," You look like a checkerboard."

Vic nodded. "I did it on purpose. If we get tired of chess, we can play checkers on my shirt."

Finding it funny, Jeffrey howled with laughter. "That's crazy."

"Then you better get ready to win at chess when I've had some of these delightful looking eggs."

After breakfast, they played two games of chess. Jeffrey was yet to beat Vic yet insisted he didn't want Vic to let him win. He knew if he ever pitched a fit at losing, it would be the end of their chess games. Instead, he gritted his teeth and pushed on. His tenacity would, one day, reward him. His strategies became more advanced with every match.

After two games that took them an hour and a half to play, Vic called for a break. He told Jeffrey, "Go see if Grandma needs any help. If not, you should go outside and get some fresh air."

"I'm getting better at chess, aren't I?"

"You sure are. If I don't play carefully, you're going to beat me."

Jeffrey went off with a grin to find Abby. She was in the dining room polishing silverware for Christmas dinner.

"I want things to look nice when you and your mom come over," she said.

"Why do you have to do that? Jeffrey asked.

Abby pointed to the pile of spoons lying on the cloth.

"See how shiny these are? They've been polished. Now look at this one."

She held up a teaspoon from the felt-lined box.

"It's darker," Jeffrey said.

"Once I polish them all, they'll all be bright."

"Would it be okay if I polish some of them?" he asked.

"Of course. Let me show you how and then I'll give you a pile of forks."

Jeffrey put all of his energy into scrubbing a shine onto the forks."

"I usually do this before Thanksgiving, but this year, we spent it out of town with our daughter and grandkids."

"I wish I was your real grandkid."

Abby's heart went out to the boy. "Honey, you are our real grandkid. We adopted you, remember. We love you just like the other kids."

Jeffrey's eyes filled with tears that he quickly brushed away. "I love you and Grandpa, too."

Abby patted his hand. "I know you do."

They worked companionably for a while before she asked Jeffrey, "Do you have any friends you're missing over break?"

He shook his head. "The guys at school don't like me. I do mean stuff and hit them. I have to go to a special room at school."

"If you don't say mean things or hit, you could be in class with the other kids. They would like you, then. You can practice making friends at the Boy's and Girl's Club."

"I will. I'm gonna be really good there. I don't want to go back to Ruby's."

"You can be really good. You do it here with Grandpa and me."

"I want you to like me and let me come over."

Abby patted his hand. We'll always like you, honey."

Jeffrey kept polishing his forks with a big smile on his face.

After lunch, he rode his bike around the cul-de-sac and climbed the large pine tree in Abby and Vic's front yard.

At one -thirty, Lauren came to pick him up for his doctor appointment. When she rang the doorbell, Abby let her in. "Jeffrey is playing outside. I'm not supposed to tell you where he us, but you should look up."

Lauren squinted at the top bare branches of the tree. "There you are, you scamp."

"I'm a good ninja. You didn't see me."

"Yes, you're a good ninja."

Lauren told Abby. "Everything is ninja now. He prides himself on creeping up on me."

Abby chuckled. "I imagine that's startling at times."

Lauren winked at Abby." I usually hear him.

Jeffrey climbed down from the tree. "I played chess with Grandpa. I lost every game, but I'm getting better. Grandpa says someday I'll be able to beat him."

Lauren ruffled his hair. "I'm the meantime, just have fun."

"I do," he assured her.

"Good. It's time to get in the car for your appointment."

Jeffrey rubbed his foot in the dirt. "Dr. Willis is boring."

Abby said, "Tell your mom what you did with the silverware today."

"Okay."

"See you tomorrow," Lauren told Abby. She gave the older woman a brief hug.

"Let me know what the doc says."

"Will do. You're a lifesaver," Lauren said.

She hustled to the car and slid behind the wheel."

"It's nice and sunny. Did you play outside a lot today?" she asked Jeffrey.

"In the afternoon I did."

Jeffrey sniffed. "It smells like popcorn. Did you bring me some?"

"I did. It's in my bag. They were giving it away at work today."

Jeffrey dug into the blue cloth bag Lauren took to work and drew out a paper bag of popcorn. He stuffed a handful into his mouth. "This is good," he mumbled. "I'm hungry."

"I bet Grandma fed you a good lunch."

"Yeah but that's was a long time ago."

"At least three hours, huh?"

She was teasing, yet Jeffrey nodded vigorously.

"It was. I had an apple before I came out."

At the rate he was eating, Lauren expected he'd grow two inches in the next two months. He already stood only four inches below her five-foot four height. His dad was over six feet so it was likely Jeffrey would be a tall guy someday. Hopefully, that's all he'd inherit. Jason had turned out to be a cheat and habitual liar. She'd worried that Jeffrey's behavioral issues had been caused by fights he'd heard between Jason and herself. Yet he'd only been a year old when Jason moved out. Surely that was too young to have suffered trauma from the confrontations she'd had with Jason.

Lauren had always been hard on Jeffrey about telling the truth. As far as she knew, he was honest, sometimes painfully so. He would be nothing like his dad, who died last year in a drunk-driving accident, and he was the drunk driver. Fortunately, he hadn't killed anyone else. He was alone in the car when he wrapped it around a tree.

At the next intersection, she turned off the main road onto a side road leading to the clinic. Lauren turned onto the street and passed a dentist's office, a laundry service, a real estate office, and the clinic. She parked in the gravel lot and shut off the car.

"I don't want to do this," Jeffrey said when Lauren opened her car door. This scene had played out so many times she knew it by heart. When he was five years old, she had to carry him in while he was screaming. When he got a little older, she had to begin to take away privileges until he slammed into the office in a rage. It took the doctor an hour to calm him down and get him to talk.

She braced herself to see what he would do today. He stared forward for a moment and then said, "I'm not going to throw a fit. Grandma and Grandpa would be disappointed in me. You might not let me go over there anymore. Still, I don't like coming here."

Lauren let out the breath she'd been holding.

They walked up the winding sidewalk and through the glass front door.

Inside, the receptionist gave them a wary look as though sterling herself for the ruckus. When it didn't happen, she said, "I'll let the doctor know you're here."

They flipped through magazines until the doctor called them back. When they'd settled on the cozy couch across from the doctor's swivel chair with large desk behind him, he asked, "How have things been going?"

"Really well," Lauren said.

"How wonderful." He raised a brow."

He focused on Jeffrey. "How do you think you're doing?"

"A lot better. I don't have mad fits anymore."

"That's great. How did that happen?"

"I can't stay with Grandma and Grandpa if I lose my temper. I don't want to stay with Ruby anymore. I want to go to the Boy's and Girl's Club. They won't let me come if I'm not good."

"It sounds like you're making real progress. I'll talk to you for a while, Jeffrey, and then your mom."

After Lauren left the room, Dr. Willis asked Jeffrey, "You've managed your temper during Christmas break?"

"At first, I'd take a breath and count to ten. Then I'd remind myself I'd be sorry. It was hardest at school and at Ruby's house. The kids in my class at school are like I was. They kick and hit and scream at everyone. Ruby ignored me or said I was being lazy or bad. Grandpa and Grandma are nice. They do things with me. They don't do things to make me mad."

"Remember what I've told you for so long?"

"Yes. Nobody can make me mad. It's a choice I make when I let them have control over me."

"That's right. It's a choice you made. Since you're choosing differently, we may be able to get you into a regular classroom. Would you like that?"

Jeffrey thought for only a second. "I would like that. I won't yell at anyone."

"It's a deal. You don't yell or fight with any of the kids and I'll try to get you back in."

"Thanks. Maybe I'll make friends to ride bikes with or climb trees. I'm training to be a ninja so I'm getting real good at hiding and being sneaky."

Dr. Willis smiled. "I'll remember that in case I can't find you. You wait out for a bit and I'll talk to your mom."

"Okay."

Jeffrey slipped out of the office to sneak up on Lauren. Though she was reading a magazine, she caught the door opening from the corner of her eye.

She smiled at him. This was the first time Jeffrey had not looked like an erupting volcano when he exited the office.

"How did it go?" she asked.

"How did you see me?" he asked. He sounded disappointed in his skill.

Lauren told him the truth. "I saw the door open."

Jeffrey considered the information a moment and said, I'll have to work on it. Also, Dr. Willis wants to see you"

"You stay here and read while I go inside. She gestured at the children's table that held kids' magazines. I'll be right back. Read something while I'm with the doctor, and don't wander off.

She nodded at the receptionist. "Lori will let me know."

"I won't. I'll stay here."

Lauren never felt totally secure leaving Jeffrey alone. Yet, this time, she believed him. She talked to the doctor who assured her Jeffrey had made a breakthrough.

"He's on the right track," the doctor said. "If he has a set-back he'll be so disappointed in himself he'll get back on track."

"I guess he finally had enough incentive to change."

"He's getting older, too. I told you there was a chance he'd outgrow it."

Tears came to Lauren's eyes. "Now is the first time since he was a baby that I can enjoy his company without being on edge. Any little thing could set him off. Not lately, though. I pray it lasts."

"From my experience, if he decides he likes himself better this way, it will last. He may have a setback here and there."

Lauren smiled at the doctor. "Thank you for all you've done."

He shook her hand. "You're a good mom to him. Keep supporting him in his efforts."

"I will."

She and Jeffrey walked out into bright afternoon sunshine, that made Lauren want to capture a mental picture of the trees in light. The verdant green of pines contrasted with the azure blue of the cloudless sky. The still, cold, air enveloped them in a cocoon that encased them in dry stillness as they crossed the gravel to the car. They took it with them until warmth from the heater dispelled it.

"Dr. Willis is going to help me get into a regular class. I hope the kids aren't scared of me. They used to be scared of me."

"I know, honey. If you've changed, they'll change too and start to trust you."

"I can wait for that because I really want some friends, the kind I see on television shows."

"Stay patient and it will happen."

As they reached their house, the bright sky faded pale like old blue eyes and a breeze stirred the branches of the cedar that sat in the front yard. They had never trimmed the branches and now the tree looked like an enormous toy top. It was the one spiked tree on the block that Jeffrey made no attempt to climb.

Inside the hallway, warmth blanketed them and took the chill from their bones. Beef stew that Lauren started in the Crockpot that morning filled the air with the scent of hearty beef, onion, tomatoes, and gravy.

THE NEXT MORNING PRODUCED six inches of snow before seven o'clock. Jeffrey stared at the glittering splendor until he could still see it when he closed his eyes. Spending the day with the grandparents was going to be marvelous. He'd build them a snowman in the front yard. If mom had carrots, he would take one for the nose. He gave thought to eyes and a mouth. He usually used sticks for the mouth and rocks for the eyes. Today's snow called for something different. They had chocolate cake donuts in the pantry. Two of them would do well for eyes. For the mouth, he would try an overripe banana he'd seen on the counter.

Mom stuck her head in the doorway and interrupted his thoughts.

"Get dressed and come in for breakfast. We've got to shovel the driveway before I leave for work."

"Ok. Can I have hot chocolate for breakfast?"

"Yes, but everything will be hot in five minutes."

"I'll hurry. I want to build a snowman in Grandma and Grandpa's yard after you leave."

Lauren smiled all the way to the kitchen. He was a different kid than he'd been when she'd been dragging him to Ruby's house. He couldn't wait to see the grandparents.

A few minutes later, he appeared. He'd dressed warmly in jeans and a flannel shirt. They sat in the chilly kitchen sipping hot cocoa and oatmeal. It wasn't his favorite cereal. Today, with snow on his mind, he didn't complain.

After breakfast, they tackled the driveway. The snow had quit falling early in the morning and begun to soften. Clearing it took almost an hour since Jeffrey kept stopping to make snowballs to throw at the snow laden tree branches.

"It looks like the tree is snowing." He laughed each time he made a throw.

"Back to work," Lauren told hm.

He'd work until the urge hit him to do it again. Finally, the driveway was clear. That would keep it from getting icy if it melted and froze again.

She dropped Jeffrey at Abby and Vic's house and headed on to work.

Jeffrey told Abby, "I'll shovel your driveway. Otherwise, you might fall if it gets slippery. If you break a bone it might not heal very fast.

That's what mom said and that I should clear your driveway. I was going to do it anyway."

Abby hugged him. It felt nice. She was warm and she smelled sweet like flowers. He wanted to remember her scent forever. When she let go, Jeffrey asked, "Where's Grandpa?"

"He's in the kitchen finishing a fresh cinnamon roll. Would you like one?"

"You bet! Mom made me oatmeal. I ate it but I don't like it."

She put her arm around his shoulder. "Let's get some before Grandpa eats them all."

"That would make him sick," Jeffrey said.

"I don't know. He looked awfully hungry."

The kitchen table held a plate of at least ten cinnamon rolls. They were fat and fluffy with tons of white icing drizzling down the sides. It smelled like cinnamon and yeast and made his mouth water.

Grandma put a plump roll on Jeffrey's plate and passed the butter. Jeffrey ran a generous knife full across the top. He took a bite and the warm roll melted in his mouth.

"Wow. This is really good. You're the best cook in the whole world."

"Thank you." Abby smiled at the compliment.

Vic took a sip of coffee to wash down his roll. "Wait until you taste the Swedish tea ring Grandma makes for Christmas morning. It will blow you away."

Vic kissed three fingers and blew into the air to show how good the tea ring would taste.

"I've never had that before."

Vic took the last sip of his coffee and told Jeffrey. "You're in for a treat."

When he couldn't eat another bite, Jeffrey said. "I wish Mom made these every day for breakfast."

Abby wrinkled her brow. "I don't think you'd enjoy them as much if you had them every day."

Jeffrey looked thoughtful. "I might."

Vic said, "The Swedish tea ring is a lot like these. Only better."

Jeffrey's eyes widened. "Wow."

As they rose from the table, Vic asked Jeffrey, "Are you ready to clear the driveway so Grandma can go to the store?"

"Sure. I cleared mine with Mom this morning."

"Let's go for two if you're not too tired."

"I'm not."

"If you have an extra snow shovel, we can work together," Vic said.

"Sure. I'll run grab it."

Jeffrey slid into his jacket and dashed out the front door. He was back in less than five minutes with the shovel. While Abby cleaned the kitchen Vic and Jeffrey began shoveling the part of the double driveway where Abby would pull out of the garage.

The dazzling brightness of the snow made it feel as if the whole world had gone white. The house, the street, and the trees were all painted white.

When he told Vic, the old man asked, "Have you ever heard of snow blindness? It happens when someone has stared at snow too long. Everything looks like a blur of light."

"It feels weird. Does it happen to you?"

"It happens to everyone if they stare at it too long."

Jeffrey worked continuously. Every now and then, Vic would take a break. Jeffrey didn't mind. Grandpa was old. He got tired fast.

When they'd cleared half the driveway, Vic went inside and told Abby she could leave. When he came back out, she'd already opened the garage. As she pulled out of the driveway, she blew each of them a kiss.

They waved as she started down the street. Vic's mouth watered at the thought of the holiday dinner she would cook. All of his favorites. He always ate too much and had to take his antacid. Yet he could never seem to stop himself. She would have sizzling turkey with a crispy brown top and his favorite cranberry salad with rolls and beans. The scent permeated his senses even though it was all in his head.

A wave of dizziness swept over him like a powerful wave that would drown him. Pain shot through his chest. He couldn't breathe. The wave was pulling him under into murky deep water, and then, he felt nothing.

When the old man went down, Jeffrey screamed, "Grandpa! He shook him by the shoulder, but Grandpa wouldn't open his eyes or speak.

Jeffrey looked wildly around the neighborhood. He didn't have a phone and the grandparents didn't have a landline. What was he going to do?"

The lady next door opened the garage and pulled her car out. Jeffrey ran to stop her.

"Wait. Please. Something's wrong with Grandpa."

Krista's hand flew to her throat and her eyes widened when she saw the old man lying in the snow. She dropped her keys beside the car and plowed across her snowy front yard into the yard next door where the elderly man lay face down on the driveway.

"Help me turn him over," she told Jeffrey.

Together they rolled Vic onto his back. Krista checked for a pulse and finding none, told Jeffrey to call 9-11.

"I don't have a phone," he stammered.

She slung her purse towards him. "There's one in my purse."

As he began digging for the phone, Krista felt Vic's neck for a pulse. Finding none, she began cardiopulmonary resuscitation.

Jeffrey found the phone. He squatted beside Krista and pushed "emergency" on the bottom left of the phone. He got the operator and said. "Grandpa was shoveling snow when he fell down, and now, he isn't moving. We need help."

The woman on the other end asked, "Is the victim conscious? "

"No. I don't think he's breathing. The lady next door is pushing on his chest."

"Okay. Tell me your location."

Jeffrey shook so hard he could barely talk, yet he managed to give her Vic's house number. Moments later, the woman on the other end said, "Stay on the line. An ambulance is on the way."

As the minutes dragged by, Jeffrey wondered how long it would be before they got help. This elderly man had become Jeffrey's best friend. He couldn't lose him now.

Though his exposure to church had been recent, Jeffrey prayed for Vic as he clutched the phone and watched Krista do compressions. Though it seemed forever it was less than ten minutes when he heard the piercing scream of the vehicle.

Jeffrey stood up and flagged them down. They parked in front of the house and spilled from the vehicle.

Krista was breathing hard when she stepped aside to let them take over. The driver, a young man, mid-twenties, with dark hair and clear blue eyes, asked Krista, "How long since this started."

Krista looked at Jeffrey, who nodded at her and said, "Right after she came out of the house."

"Ten minutes, maybe fifteen," Krista said.

"Are you two family?" the young attendant asked.

"No, just neighbors," Krista said.

"The next question was, "Is he married?

"Yes. He has a wife," Krista said.

She turned to Jeffrey. "Is she inside?"

Jeffrey shook his head, "She went shopping?"

"Can you reach her?" the man asked.

"Her number might be on his phone," Krista said.

Instead of more questions, the two attendants readied the defibrillator. Krista drew Jeffrey aside to wait under the towering pine tree. "Come over here. You won't want to watch."

"What are they going to do?"

"They're using the electric paddles to shock his heart to begin beating regularly."

One paramedic was an older man. He was shorter than the driver and had graying hair at the temples. He shouted, "Clear."

Despite her efforts to keep Jeffrey from witnessing the scene, he turned away from Krista to see Vic's chest rise above the ground at the first attempt to revive him.

"Again," the older paramedic ordered. He applied the paddles and Vic's body rose again like a marionette on a string.

"We've got a steady pulse, the younger man reported.

"Let's load, "His partner trotted off to get the stretcher.

Grandpa opened his eyes and mumbled, "What's going on?"

"You passed out," Krista said. "These guys are taking you to the hospital to see what's wrong."

He tried to sit up and the attendants pushed him gently back. Without the strength to resist, he sank onto the stretcher and met Jeffrey's frightened stare."

"I'll be okay, son."

As they locked him in place in the ambulance, he rasped," Where's Abby?"

"She's not back yet," Jeffrey told him.

He'd been walking beside the stretcher holding Grandpa's hand. He had to let go when they put Grandpa into the ambulance.

"We'll call Abby for you. Is her number in your phone?" Krista asked.

Vic nodded as they put the oxygen mask over his nose and mouth. He fumbled in his pants pocket to slip it out. The younger attendant helped him retrieve it and handed it to Krista

"We'll call her," Krista promised.

She asked Jeffrey, "Is your mom home?"

Jeffrey shook his head. "She won't be home until tonight. I stay with Grandpa and Grandma during the day."

"We'll call your mom," Krista said. "I'm a nurse and I'm headed to the hospital. Is there anyone else who could watch you?"

Jeffrey shook his head. "No, no one. I want to go to the hospital."

Krista tried to think what to do. "I can't watch you. I have to work. Maybe the volunteers at the front desk can keep an eye on you until your mom comes."

"Okay. I want to go now"

"Let me just call Abby."

Krista used Vic's phone to find Abby's number. She answered on the third ring. Krista took a deep breath and said, "I don't want to upset you, but Vic passed out in the front yard. Jeffrey found him and I called an ambulance. They're taking him to Rosedale Hospital. We can meet you in the emergency room.

Abby gasped, and then asked." Is he going to be all right?"

Krista knew from experience to never promise a loved one would be fine. If it turned out they weren't, the person who promised was blamed.

Instead, Krista said, "I don't know. He was awake and talking to us and that's a good sign."

"Tell him I'll be right there."

"I'll do that." Krista didn't tell her the ambulance was already gone. Hopefully, Vic would be well enough to talk to her when she got there. He would be getting blood work and other assessments to determine if he had suffered a heart attack. If so, the doctor would be deciding on how to treat it.

Jeffery hopped into the front seat and they started to the hospital. Krista handed him the phone to call his mom. When she answered, he told her what had happened.

"Oh, honey. I'm so sorry," she said. "I'll be right there to get you."

"I don't want to leave. I want to stay here and see how Grandpa is doing."

"Okay. We can stay a while. Where will you be when I get there?"

Jeffrey looked at Lauren for the answer.

"Tell her you'll be at the entrance with the receptionist."

After he told her, Lauren said, "You wait right there. I'm leaving."

Jeffrey handed the phone back to Krista and stared out the window. Krista's

heart ached for the child. He looked as dismal as the heavy, thick, clouds that were moving in, blotting out the sunshine that always seemed cheerful and hopeful to Krista. Dark clouds put her on edge as though they were harbingers of bad news, chasing away happy thoughts.

They made slow progress since the morning traffic bogged down at each light. Shoppers were out in full force. They passed the mall to see a sea of cars filling every space of the lot. She suspected most were looking forward to Christmas with their loved ones. For others, holidays were not easy. Memories of those who were no longer present filled them with sadness. She hoped Abby would not be one of those grieving for a missing family member this year.

She glanced at Jeffrey to see tears rolling down his cheeks. He said, "Grandpa has to get well. He's my best friend. If God lets him die, I'll be mad forever. It's not fair to give me a best friend and then take him away."

Krista struggled for words. "It may not seem fair, but it's where trust comes in. God doesn't allow bad things just to hurt us or be mean. It's hard to understand why he may take Vic. However, someday, we will understand."

Jeffrey shook his head. "I won't ever understand."

Krista sought a way to help the boy.

"Maybe we should pray for him," she said.

Jeffrey perked up. "We should. At Sunday school, the teacher says God always hears our prayers."

"He always answers them, too. Either it's yes, no, or later."

"Pray God will say yes."

"Okay, I will."

She sent a silent plea to God."

Frowning, Jeffrey said, "When are you going to start?"

Startled, she realized he expected her to pray aloud.

His plea surprised her. She hadn't planned to say a vocal prayer. She admired people who could do it, though the idea had always made her tremble. Now, Jeffrey was expecting to hear her prayer.

"I prayed in my head," she said.

"Pray out loud so I know what you're asking," he said.

She took a deep breath and plunged ahead. "Lord, you know we're worried about Vic. Please heal him. He's important to so many people. We love him and want him to come home."

When she stopped, warmth and peace washed over her like a cozy blanket on a cold day. No matter what happened next, she felt deep trust.

Jeffrey gave a shuddering sigh and wiped away his tears "He's going to be okay."

Krista knew his stoic demeanor would evaporate if there was bad news at the hospital.

She parked in staff parking and hurried with Jeffrey across the crosswalk that led to the four- story, gray-brick, regional hospital that served the community's health needs.

The automatic doors parted to welcome them into the warmth of the reception area. A middle-aged woman named Kelly greeted them. She looked over the edge of her wire-rimmed glasses and her green eyes softened when Krista told her what happened.

"This is Jeffrey. He was shoveling snow with his elderly friend, Vic, when Vic collapsed in the yard. I performed artificial respiration and he regained consciousness when the ambulance arrived. He was watching Jeffrey while his mother works. Could Jeffrey sit with you until we get his mother here?"

"Of course. Sit right here, honey." Kelly patted the chair beside her.

Jeffrey hesitated. "Can't I go with you?" he asked Krista.

"No, honey. I have to go to work. Your mom can help you find out how Vic is doing."

He sighed. "Okay."

Krista glanced back at him as she hurried to the operating room. Poor kid. As soon as she got to the scrub room, she would check the schedule and then call over to the emergency room and check the status of Vic.

Fortunately, being late had not been a problem. They were waiting on the doctor for a scheduled appendectomy. This gave her time to check on Vic. She called the in-hospital number and got Louise at the admissions emergency room desk. Krista told her the name of the patient.

After a moment, Louise came back on the line. "They're running tests. Get back with me in a half-hour and I should know more."

Krista thanked her. She wouldn't have a chance to find out more until she got a break between surgeries. She repeated the prayer for Vic she had said in the car and for comfort for Abby and Jeffrey.

CHAPTER THIRTEEN

Abby's palms were so damp she could hardly keep them on the wheel. She prayed aloud over and again, "Lord, please let him be okay. I'm not ready to lose him."

She reached the emergency room with that prayer still on her lips. Her hand shook as she opened the door and stepped into the emergency room. She had to know if Vic would be all right, yet she was terrified to ask.

She approached the front desk and the young woman looked up from the computer screen.

"How can I help you?"

Abby swallowed hard. "My husband, Victor Avery, was brought in after he went unconscious in our front yard. Can you tell me how he is doing?"

The receptionist clicked a few keys and said, "Mr., Avery is in room two. They have been running some tests. I'll call back there and see if you can come in."

"Thank you. The young woman unlocked the door to the left of her desk, Abby waited until she heard a click before she twisted the doorknob and stepped thorough the doorway into the octangular room that housed the nurses 'station and the rooms that surrounded it. Abby passed the counter of the nurses 'station. She walked past room one on her right, and then, room two.

From the doorway, she could see Vic lying in bed. Lines snaked around him leading to machines. His powder-blue eyes looked sunken in his pale face that was nearly the color of the pillow. Even though his pallor attested to his exhaustion, he smiled when she entered the room.

Her knees felt weak. None the less, she forced them to carry her over to his bed. He reached out for her hand.

"I passed out, Abby. They think it was my heart."

"I know, honey. You're going to be okay now. The doctors will find a way to help you."

"They're taking me for another test in a few minutes. I don't know what they'll find. I want you to know that I love you."

Her heart doubled its beat. He was talking like he didn't think he would recover. Her apprehension became so strong she could hardly breathe. They had been together so long that she didn't want it to end.

Two nurses entered the room. One was young with dark hair pulled into a bun. Her name tag identified her as Lori. The other nurse was middle-aged with short red hair and a soothing voice. She told Abby, "Don't worry. We're going to take good care of him and do a couple of tests to see what's wrong. He'll be back soon. You can sit in the waiting room and one of us will come out and tell you what they found."

As they pulled up the side bars, he told Abby. "Call Lauren and make sure Jeffrey is all right. The poor child was there when I passed out. He was upset when I came to and the ambulance was there."

"I'll call Lauren and make sure he's okay."

She watched as they rolled him from the room. She stood in the bay until he disappeared behind two automatic doors. Then she returned to the waiting room to wait for a nurse to tell her the tests were completed.

The clock hands moved slowly for the next hour. Abby had no idea what they were doing. Finally, the young, dark-haired nurse named Lori came out and squatted beside the chair where Abby sat. She put her hand gently upon Abby's hand and said, "Your husband has a blockage in his right coronary artery. The cardiologist is doing a stent insertion that will relieve the blockage. It's a common procedure and your husband will be placed be in a room in the coronary care unit. You can go up there to be with him when he gets there."

Abby held on to her hand. "He's going to be all right?"

Lori answered, "Better than he's been in a while. His heart will be able to get blood flow through that artery."

"Thank you, dear. The news is not as bad as I was afraid," Abby said.

"You're welcome. Try not to worry."

Lori stood and smiled at Abby before heading to the door and disappearing. Abby sat alone. Tears of relief wet her eyelashes and slid down her cheeks. She wiped them with a tissue and silently thanked God for news that Vic could be helped.

Abby called Lauren's number and told her what had happened. "He's going to be in the coronary care unit. I don't know for how long. They say he'll be better than he was before."

"That's good news," Lauren said.

Abby heard Jeffrey say, "I want to stay at the hospital with Grandma. That way I'll know how Grandpa is doing."

"You can't. I have to get back to work. You'll have to stay with Ruby for a while.

"I can stay with Grandma," he insisted.

"No. She has enough to worry about without watching you."

"I won't be any trouble."

"No, Jeffrey. You can't go into Grandpa's room. You'd be in the waiting room all alone. So, you can't be up there right now

Jeffrey's voice rose. "I want to see him. I won't be any trouble."

Lauren said, "No. He just came out of a heart procedure. So, don't you dare throw a fit."

There was a pause in which Abby tensed, worried Jeffrey would regress.

Then, she heard him say, "I don't throw fits anymore. I'll go to Ruby's, but I want to see Grandpa soon."

"You will", Lauren said.

Then she spoke to Abby. "I'm sorry. I forgot you were still on the line. I hope we didn't upset you."

"You didn't. Please tell Jeffrey I'm proud of him and how he controlled himself. We'll see you both soon."

After they finished speaking, Abby called her daughters to tell them about their dad. Neither answered. So, she left messages.

Linda called back first and said, "I got your message. What's wrong with Dad?"

"He had a heart attack, honey. They're doing a procedure to unclog his artery."

"Do you think he's going to be okay?

"I hope so, honey. He's with the doctors now. They say the stint will fix his problem."

They spoke a few more minutes and hung up with the promise from Abby to give Linda a call when she had more information.

Moments later, Julie. called. Though both girls were shocked and deeply affected, Julie broke into tears.

"What's going to happen? Will he be all right?"

"I really think so, honey. They do these all the time."

"Still, it's Dad." Her voice broke again.

When Abby had told her all she knew about what had happened to Vic," Julie said, "You'll keep me updated on how he's doing, right?"

"Of course, honey. Don't worry."

Abby wondered that she could calmly give her daughter advice not to worry when she was struggling to control her fear. Even though she prayed, the doubts crept back in.

After she hung up with Julie, she called the church to get Vic on the prayer chain. Amy answered on the first ring.

"Hi, Amy. This is Abby."

"Hi, Abby.

"Vic's in the hospital. He had a heart problem and they're putting in a stint."

"Oh, goodness honey. Don't you worry. He'll be good as new. My brother had one done two years ago and he's in great shape."

"That makes me feel so much better. I wasn't there when it happened, but he passed out in the yard. Thank God the neighbor boy was there."

"God' watching out for you and Vic," Amy said.

"I know. I shouldn't be so scared, yet I am."

"God understands that we're human."

They chatted a moment and then hung up. Abby flipped through a magazine and watched the elevator until the doors opened and a man rolled Vic into the hallway.

Abby nearly tripped in her hurry to get to him.

He took her hand and smiled. "It's amazing what they can do these days."

When they got to the doorway of his room, Abby waited while they wheeled him in and helped him onto the bed. Then, she went inside to be with him. She kissed him gently on the lips and he reached up to touch her face.

"How are you feeling, honey," she asked.

"I feel fine, tired, though."

"You gave us a scare. I'm glad Jeffrey was with you. He shouted to Krista for help and called an ambulance. He's been worried about you."

"He's a good boy. I hope he's not too upset."

"He'll be okay if you are. He loves you like a grandfather."

Her words made Vic smile.

For an hour, she held Vic's hand while he dozed. When the doctor came in, she roused Vic.

"The doctor's here, honey."

Dr. Echer appeared to be in his fifties, tall and graying, with blue eyes that seemed to smile when he greeted Abby. He introduced himself and shook her hand. "Your husband is fortunate that a nurse was near-by to give CPR."

"She's our neighbor."

Vic opened his eyes and Dr. Echer greeted him. "How are you feeling? Any pain?"

"Not too bad. A little in the top of my left leg"

"That's normal. It's where I inserted the tiny needle into your blood vessel. I'll order pain meds to keep it under control. You did really well during the procedure."

He turned to Abby and said, "Your husband watched the angioplasty while I was guiding the catheter to the blockage and he watched me put in the stent. The procedure sucked out the clot that was there. The rest of his heart looked fine."

"I'm so grateful," Abby said, "Maybe he'll have more energy. He's felt tired for weeks."

Dr. Echer nodded. "He will probably feel lots better after he recovers. If he does okay, he'll be able to go home before Christmas."

Abby squeezed Vic's hand. "Did you hear that? You could be home before Christmas."

"I'd like that," Vic said.

When the doctor left, Abby told Vic, "I didn't think you would get to go home that soon. You must be doing well."

Vic took her hand again, kissed it, and fell back asleep.

Later, when dusk was falling, Vic ate a supper of grilled chicken and vegetables while Abby went downstairs to the cafeteria to get a meal. Someone knocked on the door. He figured it was either a nurse or someone from church.

"Come in," he said.

The young woman who lived next door stepped inside. He remembered her name was Krista and that she had been there when the paramedics loaded him into the ambulance.

"How are you feeling Mr. Avery?"

"I feel well and grateful to be alive. I might not be if not for you and Jeffrey."

"I'm glad we were there and that you weren't alone. I believe there was a reason I walked out when I did and that I was supposed to help you."

"I agree with you," Vic said. "Some things are not a coincidence."

She nodded. "I don't want to keep you from resting. I just wanted to check in on you."

"You are most welcome anytime. Have you finished your shift?

"Yes. I just got done," Krista said.

Vic shifted to get more comfortable and said, "You must be tired from work, but I want you to come for dinner one night so Abby and I can get to know you better. I'm supposed to go home before Christmas. Are you free on Christmas Day?" Jeffrey and his mom will be there."

"That's very sweet. I'll be with my parents and a friend that day. My parents have a brunch and early supper. We'll try and stop by after supper."

He beamed with delight. "Abby and I have been lonely at Christmas some years. This won't be one of them."

Krista returned his smile. "I'm happy about that. Try and get some good rest tonight."

"I'm sure I will."

Abby returned a few minutes after Krista left. Apparently, they hadn't passed at the elevator. Vic told Abby about inviting her on Christmas Day. She patted his hand. "You're getting to be a socialite."

He nodded. "Yes, I am. Who's to say an old man can't have young friends?"

"Not me. I like your new friends."

Twilight deepened to winter darkness and a nurse came in to ask Abby if she was spending the night. Abby replied, "Yes, I am. I wouldn't sleep at all if I weren't here with him."

The young woman said, "It's sweet to see a couple devoted to each other. I got married a few months ago. I hope my husband and I are like you two when we're your age."

Abby said, "It takes downright stubbornness and a heap of forgiveness."

The sweet, faced girl's green eyes softened." I'll remember that."

With that said, she pulled out the bottom of the chair to turn it into a bed. She found linens, a pillow, and a blanket in a cabinet and put them on the bed. After she finished, she said, "You should be cozy now."

Abby thanked her, impressed by her sweet disposition. By now, the dim lighting gave the room a sleepy dimension. The serene landscape prints of farmlands and mountain valleys had darkened into night scenes. Vic had fallen asleep, so Abby snuggled into her pull-out bed and slept away the stress of the day.

In the morning, she awoke when a middle-aged nurse greeted Vic with a cheery "Good-morning. I'm here to get your vitals."

Abby blinked. Surprised she'd slept through the night. Sunlight streamed through the large window to her left. The landscape prints were lit again as sunlight streamed across them. The mountain stream with the running water looked so real she could imagine she was really there in that peaceful place.

The nurse took his vitals and said, "You're looking good, Mr. Avery. The doctor will be coming in a bit. He will decide if you're good to go."

"Today?" Abby asked.

The nurse smiled at her. "Most patients are able to go home only hours after the procedure."

As she left the room, Abby snatched up her phone. "I'm going to let our girls know you're going home today. They'll be so happy. They were worried about you."

Vic held up his hand. "Wait until the doctor comes in. It sounds like I'll be going home, but let's make sure."

Abby set the phone back on the table beside Vic's bed. "All right, but I'm excited we'll be home for Christmas."

They watched an old western on television until an aide brought in Vic's breakfast of scrambled egg whites and toast with applesauce on the side."

"I'll be learning to cook a bit differently for you," Abby said.

"Go down and get your breakfast while I eat this," Vic said. "Maybe we can have lunch at home."

Abby went down for scrambled eggs, bacon, and a slice of toast. I'll be cutting out the bacon, so I may as well enjoy some today, she thought. When she finished and went back upstairs, the doctor was talking to Vic.

He smiled at Abby. "Your husband's heart is sounding good. I told him to watch the small wound we made for the incision. Make sure it stays clean. He should rest today and no heavy lifting. I'll see him in a week at my office."

"He can go home?" Abby asked.

"I'll write the discharge. You should be out of her within an hour."

Abby scrambled in her purse for her phone. "That's good news. Now I can tell the girls."

Vic nodded. "Now you can tell the girls."

After she called Linda and Julie, Abby helped Vic get ready to go home. An hour later armed with his new diet, they pulled into the driveway where the snow Vic and Jeffrey had been shoveling had melted. The sky was a bright, clear blue. Puffy clouds chased each other in the gentle cold breeze.

Abby let Vic settle onto his cozy chair while she grabbed the mail from their white mailbox in the front of the house. There were two bills and a late Christmas card from Vic's best friend in college. They corresponded once a year since they no longer lived in the same state. She brought the card to Vic and he smiled when he read it.

"This old boy can always make me laugh," Vic said. He showed Abby the family letter with a photo of Mitch hamming it up by lying on the floor tangled in Christmas tree lights. The photo on the back showed the tree with the lights strung every which way and the balls hanging crooked on the top of the tree. Below it, he offered to decorate a tree for anyone who wanted to hire him.

Abby chuckled as she remembered the silly pranks the two men had played on each other. It was nice their sense of humor had not dimmed as the aches and maladies of old age set in. There was something to be said for staying young at heart.

She stood back to appreciate the white artificial tree that stood in front of the picture window near Vic's big chair. The blue balls captured light from the window and sparkled bright sapphire blue. Red velvet ribbons contrasted with the white of the tree and the green garland draped gracefully around the branches.

Vic followed her gaze. "You did a beautiful job, Abby. You lend grace and beauty to everything you do, in our home, and in the outside world. I should appreciate you more."

His heartfelt compliment brought tears to her eyes.

She bent and hugged him. "I hope you know how special you are to me and how scared I was of losing you."

"An old codger like me? You could replace me."

She cupped his face in her hands and kissed him on the forehead. "Don't ever say that. I could never replace you and I'd never try."

"Good. I could never replace you, either."

They watched a little television and Vic rested until time for lunch. Abby fixed them a meal of broiled fish and steamed vegetables. She was determined to stick to the diet and keep Vic healthy.

They spent the afternoon reading. When the shadows lengthened and the sunlight no longer spilled through the window, she called Lauren to tell her Vic was home. Lauren had called the evening before when Abby had gone to the cafeteria for supper. Abby had promised to call today and update her. As expected, she was thrilled to hear Vic was home.

"Jeffrey will be excited, too. I'll try and keep him away for a while so that Vic can rest."

"Only for today. I expect both of you over for Christmas. We'll be disappointed if you don't come. The doctor said Vic can go back to normal activity. He just can't lift anything heavy for a while."

"You can always ask Jeffrey when you need help. He would be delighted to come to your aid."

"I know," Abby said. "He's a dear and we love him."

"He thinks the world of you and Vic and so do I."

"You're both special to us, too. That's why we would be disappointed if you don't come for breakfast tomorrow and gifts at the tree."

"In that case, you can be sure we'll be there. Is nine o'clock good?"

"It's perfect."

They hung up and Abby went over her breakfast menu. She would still make a Swedish tea ring, eggs, and bacon. Vic could have a slice of the tea ring. The rest of his breakfast would be scrambled egg whites and fruit.

CHAPTER FOURTEEN

The next morning, promptly at nine o'clock, Lauren and Jeffrey arrived looking frosty from the cold. No more snow had fallen Most had melted except for a few patches in the yard. Blue sky and sunshine would be theirs for Christmas Day.

"Come in. Get warm," Abby said. "There's breakfast in the kitchen."

Jeffrey beamed at her. "Mom loved the toaster you took me to get. We tried it out with a slice of toast to split and it worked great."

Abby gave him a hug. "I'm so glad."

"Where's Grandpa?" he asked.

"He's in the kitchen with a cup of hot tea. He's waiting for you to dig into breakfast."

Jeffrey made a zooming sound. "I'm on the way."

Jeffrey skittered across the floor and through the kitchen doorway. They heard Vic belt out a greeting. Lauren hugged Abby and said, "Jeffrey's been awfully worried about his friend."

"So was I. However, the doctor assures us he's doing great."

"We were thrilled to hear that," Lauren said.

The women joined Vic and Jeffrey and Abby served their breakfast of the round, yeasty, tea ring with sweet, white, icing on the top and dripping down the sides. Maraschino cherries and sliced almonds decorated the top. A platter of steaming scrambled eggs, and crispy bacon made up the sides.

Vic offered a blessing. Then Abby said, "Dig in. Eat as much as you like."

Happy chatter accompanied their breakfast. Jeffrey talked about the presents he'd opened at home. Then he squirmed in his chair as he waited for the grown-ups to finish so they could open the presents under Vic and Abby's tree.

When everyone had eaten all they could hold, they moved to the living room. Jeffrey wanted Abby and Vic to open his first.

When Abby opened the picture of their house that Jeffrey had painted, she and Vic exclaimed, "Our house!"

Abby held it up. "It's beautiful. I'll treasure this always. You did a beautiful job on it."

"You have real talent, son," Vic said.

Jeffrey beamed at their approval. "I'm glad you like it. Mom said you would."

Speaking of Mom, here's a present for her," Abby said.

Lauren opened the envelope to find the gift card to the discount store

"Thank you," she said.

"You're very welcome," Abby said.

Next, she opened the box. Inside, was nestled a soft, baby-blue, sweater. Lauren gasped and said, "It's beautiful. I can wear it under my coat to keep warm. In the spring, I'll wear it over a blouse. Thank you. This is really too much."

"Not for you, honey," Abby said.

Vic held out a present for Jeffrey.

He opened the box.

"Comic books, yeah," he shouted. "I love them."

They let him thumb through the books for a minute before Abby handed him his second gift. He opened the art set and sat staring at it dumbfounded. "It's got everything. Everything I need. This is great."

His excitement put wide grins on all the adults' faces.

"Can I open it and do a watercolor right now? Jeffrey asked.

"Let me clear the kitchen table and you can work in there," Abby said.

Lauren jumped up from her chair. "Tell me what to do and I'll help you."

While Abby and Lauren cleared the table and put away the food, Jeffrey stayed with Vic and told him about all the art he planned to produce. "Someday, I'll make paintings and people will buy them. Do you think I can?"

"It wouldn't surprise me at all," Vic said.

When the kitchen was clear, Jeffrey went to work painting. The adults collected in the living room to listen to Christmas carols and talk. It was then that Lauren shared her hopes of going back to school and studying accounting. If I could become a Certified Public Accountant, I could open my own business someday."

Abby exchanged a look with Vic. Then she said, "We'd be happy to have Jeffrey with us if you want to take some night classes."

Lauren thought it over. "I wouldn't ever want him to be a burden to you. I'm sure you are tired by evening."

"Look at the class schedules and see if there are any in the early evening. Us old codgers don't go to bed until ten o'clock. If you were back by nine, we'd be fine with that."

Lauren smiled. Her eyes lit. "I will check. Thank you."

A few moments later, the doorbell rang. Abby raised her brows and asked Vic, "Are we expecting anyone?"

"I don't think so."

She looked out the window and squealed. "It's the girls!"

"What!" Vic rose from his chair.

Abby opened the door to see Julie and Linda. They held a beautiful potted poinsettia between them. The red leaves came to perfect points above the green foliage. It was one of her favorite plants and she had lost her only other poinsettia last summer.

She accepted the plant and placed it on the table beside the door. Then she drew the girls inside and hugged them.

"This is such a wonderful surprise. You're both here at the same time. How did you do it?"

Julie said, "We flew to Denver and met for a connecting flight."

"You couldn't have given us a better Christmas present. Let's go see your dad."

Vic was already moving toward them. Linda rushed to hug him. "Sit, Dad. We'll come to you. We've been worried about you."

They hugged him gingerly as though he might break.

Jeffrey came running in from the kitchen. "What's all the noise?" he asked.

"Abby answered, "Our daughters have come to visit. It's a wonderful surprise."

"Wow. They're all grown-up," he said.

Abby chuckled. "Of course. Julie has children older than you."

Abby gestured to Lauren, who was now perched on the edge of the sofa and said, "Here's our good friend and neighbor, Lauren Murphy. She's Jeffrey's mom."

"It's so nice to meet you," Lauren said. "My son and I think your parents are the nicest people we have ever met."

"We agree with you," Linda said.

"How long can you stay?" Abby asked her girls.

"Three days," Linda answered.

Vic slapped his knee. "We'll pack all we can into it."

"Yes, but from inside the house. You're supposed to be resting," Julie said.

Vic shook his head. "No need to baby me. The doctor said I can be back to normal after today. Just no heavy lifting."

The girls looked at their mom for confirmation.

It's true," Abby said.

"Then I suppose we can drive around and look at Christmas lights tonight, like old times," Julie said.

Jeffrey whooped. "I want to go."

Lauren stood and put her hand on his shoulder. "Honey, their daughters don't get to see them often. We need to go home and let them visit."

Jeffrey's expression changed from excitement to disappointment. "I don't want to go home. It will be boring there."

"Jeffrey, this is a special time for them. You better not spoil it," Lauren warned.

Vic put his hand on Jeffrey's shoulder. "Lauren, we wouldn't think of sending you and Jeffrey home. We can all go together tonight. I'm sure Julie and Linda would like to get to know you."

"We would," Linda said. "Jeffrey saved our dad's life and you're his mom. That makes you both special to us."

"We're sure," Julie agreed.

While Jeffrey finished his picture, the adults visited in the living room."

Later, they shared an early dinner of vegetable lasagna that Abby pulled from the freezer and they ate the rest of the Swedish tea ring for dessert. Since Julie and Linda insisted on doing the dishes, they were both in the kitchen when the doorbell rang.

"Who could that be? "Abby asked.

She opened the door to see Krista and Trent and a man she didn't know standing outside.

"We wanted to stop by and wish you a Merry Christmas," Krista said.

"Please, come in," Abby told her. "You can meet our daughters. They gave us the gift of a surprise visit today."

The threesome stepped inside. Krista waved at Lauren. "With us here, it looks like you have all of your neighbors in your house."

Lauren joined them as Abby said, "You folks are some of our favorite people in the whole world and we're all together on Christmas Day. However, Trent, it seems you have brought someone we haven't met, and he looks a lot like you. Is this your brother?"

Trent grinned. "I have to admit, he's my older brother. Much older and his name is Parker."

Parker shook hands with the group. "I'm three years older and much wiser."

Linda and Julie came from the kitchen to find out who had come in. After making introductions, Linda said, "We have our very own party now. We can all carpool and look at lights. When we get back, we should watch an old Christmas movie together if everyone has time."

"If Dad's not too tired," Julie added.

"If I get tired, I'll go to bed. No reason for the rest of you to break up," Vic said.

Bored with grown-up talk, Jeffrey said, "Is it time to look at lights now?"

"Abby chuckled. "Yes. It's time, but we won't all fit in one car."

Julie said, "We can take you and Dad and Jeffrey and Lauren in your car. I don't mind driving."

"We have plenty of room," Trent said. "Jeffrey and Lauren can go with us."

"I want to go with Grandma and Grandpa. Mom, you can go with them."

"Wow. I think I'm not needed with my grown-up boy," Lauren said.

Jeffrey grinned up at her. "I love you, Mom."

She tweaked his nose. "Imp."

Jeffrey rode with the grandparents in the back seat while Julie drove, and Linda rode shotgun.

At first, Lauren felt awkward sitting in the back seat with Parker while Krista and Trent sat in the front. Yet, after Parker began a conversation with her, Lauren relaxed. He wanted to know about her job, her family, and her background.

"Have you lived here all your life?" he asked.

"No. I grew up in Sage, about two hours away."

He grinned. "I know where that is. We played your high school in baseball every year."

"Who won?" she asked.

"It was close, but our team was better."

He was teasing her.

"Oh really? I don't remember any school being better," she said.

He chuckled. "You're loyal. I like that."

He was lean and muscular, with a ready grin and smiling blue eyes a shade lighter than his brother's hat."

Lauren was intrigued by Parker. His friendliness seemed genuine as did his interest in her. Though her mind warned her to be careful, her heart would not let her deny the attraction she felt.

"Trent said you used to be a contractor here. Where do you live now?" she asked.

"I moved to a city called Benton. It's growing fast and there's a lot of new home construction. It's about three hours from here."

Lauren thought it sounded familiar "I believe we went through there when we visited my dad's relatives when I was a kid."

"It's pretty. The elevation is lower, and we have aspen and Ponderosa pines. However, we don't have skiing like you do here."

"I've never been a skier," Lauren admitted.

Parker laughed. "I haven't skied in so long that I'd probably break a leg on the bunny slope."

"My sport is more like taking long walks, though I haven't had time in the last few years."

"Your job and your son keep you busy, huh?"

Lauren nodded. "End of the year accounting is hectic and it hasn't been easy to find sitters for Jeffrey. Abby and Vic have been lifesavers."

"I think they love you both like family."

Lauren smiled. "They're special people."

Trent wound through a few more neighborhoods. Parker and Lauren paid little attention to the lights. They were caught up in their own world exploring each other's interests and lives. When they got back to Abby's house, Julie pulled her parents' car into the garage. Trent parked in the driveway. He turned to the couple in the back seat and asked, "How did you like the lights?"

"Did you see any of them?" Krista asked. "I heard a lot of talking from the back seat."

Lauren felt a blush creep into her face.

"We saw enough of them," Parker said.

When they piled out of the car to tell Abby and Vic good-night, Parker hung back with Lauren. He walked closely enough for her to catch the tangy scent of his aftershave. Lauren committed it to her memory to store when she wanted a dose of what she had felt tonight.

Before they caught up with Trent and Krista, Parker told Lauren, "I'll be in town for a couple of days. Would you and Jeffrey like to go to the ice rink on Saturday and out to lunch?"

Anticipation bubbled through Lauren's veins and warmed her on this cold night.

"We'd love to," she said.

They joined the others inside Abby and Vic's house Jeffrey told everyone who would listen about his favorite lights. After a few minutes of chatting, the group broke up. Krista and Trent went home, and Parker went back to stay with his mom.

As Lauren walked home with Jeffrey, she told him that Trent's brother had invited them for skating and lunch. Her uncertainty about his answer was assuaged when he replied, "That would be great. I wanted to skate on the pond. Grandma Abby said we had to wait until it was frozen solid. Now I don't have to wait."

Lauren smiled at his enthusiasm. She knew she would hear little else from him expect how much fun it would be to go skating. She hoped he liked Parker because she certainly did.

When Saturday arrived, Lauren and Jeffrey were ready when Parker came for them. He; looked handsome in a black leather jacket and black slacks. He smiled at Lauren and she felt the same connection as she had when they'd ridden together in the car. Their gazes locked for a long moment until Jeffrey said, "Are we going skating?"

Parker grinned at him. "We are going skating and then we're going to lunch. Have you ever skated before?"

Jeffrey shook his head. "I want to learn. Grandma Abby was going to teach me, but now she's busy taking care of Grandpa."

"How about if I teach you?" Parker asked.

"Yeah. That would be good." Jeffrey pulled on his jacket.

Parker helped Lauren into her thigh-length wool coat. It was old, yet presentable for an outdoor sport. She only hoped she would remember the little skill she had when she'd skated as a child.

"I rented the skates yesterday," he told Lauren. I hope I remembered the sizes right."

Lauren said, "If I fall down a lot, I'll tell you that you got mine wrong and use it as an excuse."

He feigned shock. "You'd blame me?"

She didn't hesitate. "Of course."

They drove `to the pond. Parker had checked to see that the sign on the post stated the pond was frozen deep enough for skating. A dozen kids and a few adults were already enjoying the ice. Jeffrey watched as a girl about his age performed a figure eight.

"Wow. That's what I want to do," he said.

Lauren and Parker exchanged amused smiles.

"That will take some practice," Lauren said.

"I'll practice every day if you'll let me," he said.

Parker grinned at Lauren. "Maybe he's a future Olympian."

She smiled back. "I don't know if he'll stick with it that long."

Lauren teetered a bit as she edged onto the ice. Jeffrey picked his way along and then fell forward on his hands and knees. "It's too slippery," he said.

Lauren laughed. "It's ice, honey."

Parker proved to have remembered his skating skills better than the other two. He took turns between them helping them glide across the pond. He put one arm around Lauren's waist and held her by the arm. His closeness gave her a thrill that surpassed that of gliding across the ice.

After two hours on the pond, Jeffrey's ankles were bending inward and refusing to support him any longer. He'd had fun, yet it was time to quit.

"Can we have burgers for lunch?" Jeffrey asked.

Parker nodded. "I know a diner that has burgers as well as plate lunches. I thought we'd go there."

"It sounds good to me," Lauren said.

It was good. She had a wonderful time talking to Parker as she ate a chicken cob salad. He was a kind and generous man and the first one who had taken an interest in Jeffrey.

They finished lunch with scoops of chocolate ice cream. When Parker dropped them home, Lauren could already feel sore muscles in her calves. She didn't mind in the least. It had been well worth it.

She missed Parker as soon as he drove away. He was leaving the next day and she would miss him. She signed and reminded herself that he'd asked if he might call her when he got home. Of course, she had agreed. As the winter progressed, Parker called often. They grew closer. On Valentine's Day, he drove down to take her to dinner. Abby and Vic kept Jeffrey, who was now adjusting well to his general education classroom and making friends there.

After dinner at the restaurant, Parker pulled out a small box. Lauren's heart raced as she guessed what was inside. She opened it to find a lovely ring with a sparkling round diamond. She looked into Parker's eyes and saw the love she had missed and longed for all the years she had been raising Jeffrey by herself. It was all that she could have asked for and all she would ever want. She knew she would never have had it if not for the relationship with her neighbors that had brought Parker into her life on a special Christmas Day.

Sign up for my newsletter for news, freebies ands fun and get a free download of my sweet contemporary romance MADE FOR EACH OTHER SCAN HERE

ABOUT THE AUTHOR

A native of Houston, TX, Karen spent her early years enjoying life along the Gulf Coast. After high school, she attended Texas A&M as well as the University of Houston where she obtained a B.S. in early childhood education. She has written numerous articles and stories, books for children, and novels for adults. She particularly enjoys writing contemporary and historical romance. She now lives in the

Southwest with her family and assorted pets.

DEAR READERS,

I appreciate the time and attention you gave in reading my book. I hope you enjoyed it. If so, would you consider leaving a review on Goodreads or your favorite download site? I would truly appreciate your time. Blessings to you and yours.

Goodreads

Don't miss out!

Visit the website below and you can sign up to receive emails whenever Karen Cogan publishes a new book. There's no charge and no obligation.

https://books2read.com/r/B-A-QNTE-LGJKB

BOOKS 2 READ

Connecting independent readers to independent writers.

Also by Karen Cogan

God's Lessons for Little Kids
Sunny Under the Sea
Chatty Clam Spreads Gossip
Hermit Finds a Home

Grandma Mandy Series
Made for Each Other
Landscape of Love
Jack of Hearts

Henry With Family and Friends
Henry Has the Hiccups
Henry's Loose Tooth

Prequel for MADE FOR EACH OTHER, GRANDMA MANDY SERIES
The Golden Summer

Standalone
The God of Apple Juice and Spilled MIlk
The God of Apple Juice and Spilled Milk Study Guide
The Prodigal Heart
Do Not Disturb
The Great Camp-Off
The Gum Chewing Ghost
Too Scared to Move
Between Best Friends
Waiting for Mama
Henry Asks
Pancho Finds A Home
If There Were Two of Me
The Flower Girl
The Flower Girl
Retribution
A Relative Matter
Katrina: Too Far From Home
Betrayal
The Neighbors

Watch for more at www.karencogan.com.